Beyond Broken Pencils
A School Shooting Tale of Heartbreak and Healing

By Julie C. Gilbert

Aletheia Pyralis Publishers

http://www.juliecgilbert.com/
https://sites.google.com/view/juliecgilbert-writer/

Love Science Fiction, Fantasy, or Mystery?

Choose your adventure!

Visit: **http://www.juliecgilbert.com/**

For details on getting free books.

Dedication:

I'd like to dedicate this book to my grandmother, Miriam.
She was a wise and loving lady.

Thank you to the friends and fans who lent me their names for this
story.
See the "Friends and Fans" page to see where you can find your
fictional namesake.
It's an honor and a pleasure to know you.

Disclaimer:
The names and situations described herein are inspired by people
I know of or have heard about, but they are scrambled
and altered in significant ways for safety and privacy.

Warning:
Most of my works are squeaky clean and suitable for all ages.
However, due to the graphic nature of the content,
reader discretion is advised.
Please stop reading immediately if it becomes too intense for you.

Friends and Fans:

A work like this requires a lot more names than most stories. The underlined portion is the real name used. In many cases, I opted only for the first names or mixed and matched.

Alycia Teller – numerous chapters, chemistry teacher
Nikki – Ch. 17, Ch. 18, chemistry teacher
Corrie Kelman – Ch. 11, biology teacher
Doc G. – Ch. 9, special education teacher
Mrs. Meyer – Ch. 4, Ch. 8, physics teacher

Tonya Gilbert – Ch. 3, student
Ms. Jayne – Ch. 5; Ian's English teacher
Ms. Finigan – Ch. 7, Ch. 9; school nurse
Carol Reese – Ch.12, Ch. 16, Ch. 21; high school drama teacher
Ms. Dalton – Ch. 17; science supervisor
Faith Moffitt – Ch. 21, Ch. 25, Ch. 34; middle school art teacher
Tess – Ch. 21, Ch. 25; 911 operator
Sean Burgess – Ch. 24, Ch. 27, Ch. 31; police officer
Jennifer Burgess – Ch. 24, Ch. 31; first-grade teacher; police officer's wife
Bonnie Kiernan – Ch. 25, Ch. 31., Ch. 33, Ch. 38-40, Epilogue, police officer
Kelly VanDaley – Ch. 26, physical education teacher
Sandie – Ch. 26, librarian
Mr. Wright – Ch. 3, Ch. 26, Epilogue, history teacher
Anabelle Lins – Ch. 26, Ch. 35, Ch. 38, Ch. 39, student
Wendy Freeman – Ch. 31, Ch. 34, Ch. 37, EMT
Becca Treddle – Ch. 34, Ch. 39, Epilogue, journalist
Dr. Hollon – Ch. 40, Ch. 41, doctor
Shauna Easterwood – Ch. 41, grandmother

Table of Contents:

Preface:

Dear Reader,

If you've been with me for any length of time, you know I strive to make every work a clean read. That said, this story cannot be told without a "disturbing content" warning, simply for the subject matter.

Every few months the major headlines will focus on the latest school shooting. If it's bad enough, such headlines will dominate the news feeds for weeks or even months. If it's not bad enough, the story will slip into oblivion in a matter of days. The place that is a focal point gets added to the ever-lengthening list of immortalized locations. As of this writing, Santa Fe and Parkland are the latest buzzwords, but it's inevitable that eventually they will be replaced by another tragedy in an endless cycle. That's not to say there haven't been other shootings since, but none with a death toll high enough to jar these two from our collective memories.

There is no simple fix or convenient scapegoat.

Broken families, depressed people, violent video games, and easy access to guns might be pieces of the puzzle, but they're certainly not the only ones. People like to key in on one or two issues, but until we can change the core of humanity, these things will continue to happen. You can try to say mass-murder of this sort is a uniquely American problem, and maybe by narrow definitions that is true. But given enough motivation people will find a way to misuse anything.

Until you deal with the heart, the mind, and the soul, evil will reign. That's kind of the hallmark of human history. Yet amidst any tragedy, you will always find heroes.

I'm a writer and a high school chemistry teacher. I've studiously avoided the topic of schools for a long time, but my hope is that within these pages, you will find both a compelling story and a reason to connect more with the people around you. Nobody flames out so spectacularly as to become a school shooter or a mass-murderer of any flavor in a void. It's an extreme cry for attention. Please don't think I'm confusing the victims here. People who perpetrate acts like this richly deserve having the entire law book thrown at them. I'm talking about preventing events from escalating to that point.

My prayer is that this fictional tragedy will one day prevent a real one. If you learn nothing else, remember this: life is precious. It can be short, painful, annoying, or seemingly hopeless, but it's worth experiencing.

Join me on this journey, and we will find the hope that lies *Beyond Broken Pencils.*

Sincerely,

Julie C. Gilbert

Liquid Prayers

One week slipped by, then almost two.
Each moment made the pain recede,
But I wanted to cry…
I wanted to cry for the angry man
Who stole so many lives.
I wanted to cry for the people
Who would never see home again.
Wanted to cry for the strangers
Mourning a loved one lost.
Wanted to pour out liquid prayers
For everyone wounded in body, spirit, and soul.

Imagine my dismay when I discovered
Something deep within holds my tears at bay.
Have I seen too much to cry?
Or is there too much to cry for?

Though no tears may come,
My heart will weep.
I will weep for the angry man,
For those who fell that day,
For everyone beyond our help.
I will weep for the strangers
Whose pain may not recede.
I will pour out liquid prayers
To bind wounds of body, spirit, and soul.

Prologue:
Two-Pencil Day

Friday, 3:07 p.m.
Brantford Regional High School
Brantford Township, New Jersey

It could have been worse. Thank goodness it was only a two-pencil day.

Naomi Harrison-Kensley packs up her junk and double-checks to make sure she hasn't forgotten anything. She always feels a little odd invading another teacher's space for a single period in the day. Pens, simple scientific calculators, the sad remains of two pencils, discarded classwork sheets, and labs that need grading get piled on top of the folders and extra worksheets already weighing the plastic bin down. Picking up the whole bundle, she opens the door, pushes through, and staggers diagonally across the hall to room 106, the work equivalent of home sweet home.

Spotting Alycia Teller at the front sink washing her hands, Naomi kicks at the door to announce her presence and desire to enter without juggling the bin-o-everything. She takes a small step back to give her friend room to swing the door open for her. Mumbling thanks, Naomi maneuvers past the giant Chromebook cart, plops the bin on the nearest desk, and perches on the first desk in the second row.

"How did the lab go today?" asks Alycia. She shuffles sideways past the first column of desks to reach the inconveniently located paper towel dispenser at the back of the room. The move causes her double ponytail to swing back and forth, emphasizing the rainbow tipped ends.

1

Glancing around, Naomi spots a student still finishing up something.

"Well, we didn't set off the fire alarms or cause any noteworthy injuries, so I guess it went well enough," she says. "One of the thermometers broke, but overall, the equipment casualty list was short today."

"Good to hear. And I appreciate the lack of fire alarm." Alycia finishes drying her hands then takes the long way around to the front teacher's desk. "I kept a sweatshirt close just in case."

"Thanks for the vote of confidence," Naomi notes dryly.

"It's not that I don't trust your kids, but I don't trust your kids," Alycia says.

Chuckling, Naomi internally admits that *she* doesn't trust her kids when it comes to certain dangerous pieces of lab equipment. Getting up, she starts fixing the Great Desk Migration. For some reason, every day the desks slowly inch to the right until there is barely room to breathe while squeezing past the first column and the lab benches located on the left side of the room as one enters.

By the time she finishes, Alycia's student has completed the work and sauntered out.

Comfortable silence falls, save for the soothing tap-tap-tap of keyboard keys.

After retrieving the remains of her lunch from the back prep room, Naomi sinks into a desk at random and munches on pretzels. Some days she has plenty of time to eat, but not B days. Covering for a teacher on maternity leave means an extra class. The randomness of the drop cycle means that one day of every four she has to teach five of the six hour-long blocks. That puts lunch at nine o'clock in the morning. Since her body doesn't function if not fed and watered at regular intervals, she's come up with the solution of locking students out between the back-to-back lab periods. The precious ten minutes leaves enough time for a potty break or a lightning-quick lunch, but that usually means some random snacks go uneaten.

"Do we have any M&M packs left?" Naomi inquires.

"Maybe," Alycia says noncommittally. She disappears behind the massive front desk and emerges a moment later triumphantly waving an M&M fun pack. "Found one. Might be slightly expired."

She hurls the candy across the room into Naomi's waiting hands.

"Thanks." Naomi promptly rips open the package and starts pairing up individual chocolate candies with mini-pretzels. "And I won't look at the date. Then, what I don't know can't hurt me."

"Not sure I agree with that logic," says Alycia. "The day must have been a doozy."

Naomi quirks an eyebrow at her friend to ask what gave her that impression.

"You're stress eating M&M's without even sorting them by color," Alycia explains.

"It wasn't bad for a B Day." Naomi lets the day scroll through her head before listing the noteworthy incidents. "A few key students were absent so 4th was positively quiet. Randy only broke two pencils this morning, and he was decent enough to bring his own instead of breaking mine this time. Dan took a nine-minute bathroom break. Connor was glued to his phone, and Dante tried to teach some of the boys how to skip out on a central detention."

"Would his method work?" Alycia wonders.

"I doubt it," Naomi answers honestly. "It hinges on having a family that doesn't care enough to back up the discipline from home." The words sadden her. She would bet her last paycheck that even Dante would trade the ability to skip out on detention for the chance to live with the rest of his family. His grandmother does her best, but she isn't exactly an energy match for a head-strong teenage boy. "It's just sad." Naomi munches on another few candy pieces and follows them with pretzels. "But Dante redeemed himself a little later by making me laugh."

"How'd he do that?"

"Called another kid 'uncultured swine.'" She smiles at the memory. "I don't even know what the rest of the conversation was about but hearing Toy Story quoted by him like that was priceless. I don't think he even knew it was a quote."

"Kids say some crazy things," Alycia points out.

"They do indeed," Naomi agrees. She shoves the uneaten remains of lunch back into her bag and puts the bag into her already-bulging backpack. Instinctively, she checks for her grade sheets. Spotting the labs in the bin-o-everything, she plucks them out and adds them to the to-grade folder. Grading likely won't happen, but she wants to be prepared anyway.

She thinks back to various conversations throughout the week. Students baffle her. One minute they're cursing up a storm, and the next, they're gushing with excitement over the latest video game or their favorite lunch menu item.

"It's been a long week," Naomi notes.

"Hey, at least it's Friday," says Alycia.

"You can say that again." Naomi walks over to her travel mug of room-temperature tea and raises it in acknowledgement. Setting the mug down again, she picks up the plastic bin and hauls it into the back prep room.

Out of sight, out of mind.

"Got anything special planned?" Naomi asks, re-entering the main room.

"Sleep. Play with the cats, visit the family. The usual," answers Alycia. "You?"

"Jack is headed to London again for the week, so I guess I'll help him pack Saturday, then drive him to the airport." Naomi frowns down at her backpack. "Ick airports. I try not to think about that part. I'd much rather he hire a car, but we're trying to save money for a house. Since tonight's movie night, that leaves the lesson-planning marathon for Sunday after church."

"Sounds fun-filled," says Alycia. "You'll be anxious to get back to work so you can relax."

"Indeed. And it's a C-week. I even get to start out with the prep period that should have been for today." Naomi shrugs. "I'll leave the bulk of the grading for then."

"Good plan." Alycia stands up and gathers her stuff. For some odd reason, the woman insists upon carrying a foot-high stack of textbooks, binders, and papers.

"We go home?" Naomi inquires.

"We go home," Alycia confirms.

They each check that they have their belongings, shut off the lights, and head out for a well-earned weekend break.

Chapter 1:
The Big Day

I killed my mother.

Ian Colt tests the thought. He could do it. He should do it. He would do it.

But not yet.

After all she put him through, she deserves to see the end results of today first. Perhaps she'd do the entire world a favor and take herself out with those pills she loves more than anything.

Forcing himself to get up, Ian rips open a Pop Tart pack and eats the pair together, hardly taking the time to taste them. After brushing his teeth and throwing on some clothes, he straightens the bed and lays out his equipment. Undertakings like this sure involve a lot of stuff.

Look, Mom. See what I can do.

The silent words have a childish ring to them inside his head. He remembers saying them many times during the good days, the pre-Little-Miss-Perfect days. Most parents can deal with having two kids, but not Sandra Marie Colt. She swings from doting mother to raging maniac in a heartbeat. Over the years, Ian has adopted a strict avoidance policy when it comes to his mother. That works most of the time. At least it did before Thad entered the picture and started meddling. He's usually all buddy-buddy, but Ian knows better. Thad doesn't really care. He just

5

needs a pet project to feel better about his sorry, fat, middle-aged self.

Twin surges of purpose and excitement course through Ian. He's never felt more alive. More than two years of planning and preparation would pay off today. He's probably bussed a thousand tables to earn the cash to build his arsenal. Maybe Thad's endless ramblings about life goals and aspirations sank in after all.

That's where his heroes went wrong.

Write nothing. Say nothing.

He can't remember exactly when the fascination with school shooters started. Middle school, probably. Miss Danbury had asked them to write an essay about somebody they admired. Ian chose Eric Harris and Dylan Klebold of Columbine fame. That had earned a trip to the principal's office, two lunch detentions, and a glorious freak-out from his mother.

Since then, he's thought a lot but written very little and typed even less. He's printed a few maps of the high school and marked out several routes, sketching stuff in the margins and on the back, but he plans to burn and flush the papers before beginning. Let them wonder about the reasons. He doesn't plan on being around this lousy world long enough to care what they think of him.

That's a lie.

He cares.

He cares very deeply.

They *will* remember him. That's the point. He's about to join a long history of school shooters, but he's going to do it better. When the thought first entered his head, Ian had considered journaling about the experience, but he decided not to waste time with childish boasts and private rants. Instead, he's become a model citizen. He is still a mediocre student, but somebody the case managers mention among their triumphs.

He doesn't need bombs to make a lasting impression, just guns. Lots of guns. Guns are beautiful weapons. A bit loud and brash, but sleek and elegant too. They can be cold and calculating, but they are also perfectly neutral. They don't judge like people do. They simply point in one direction and destroy upon command.

An AR-15 is lovingly packed into a lacrosse bag. A separate, identical bag gets stuffed into the first lacrosse bag. This bag will be used to transport the secret weapon to his gym locker. Several loaded handguns get stored in various pockets among his three backpacks. Spare magazines, power bars, and water bottles find their way into every conceivable crevasse.

Ian considers taking some videos of today to email his mother and Thad, but he resists, as he has so many times before. He also doesn't have the time. He needs to get to school on time so they don't call his mother. It wouldn't be a big deal, but she'd call him to yell and he doesn't need that kind of aggravation this morning.

He has a hit list, but only in his head. So many people deserve to die. He could start early and off Little Miss Perfect before she even wakes up, but that wouldn't make the same sort of statement. Ian needs to look into her eyes the moment he pulls the trigger. She must see it's him. That will turn her world upside down for whatever scant seconds she has left.

The Trio: Malcolm Jones, Curtis Ryman, and Max Kessler.

Those jerks have haunted Ian since elementary school. But in a way, he owes them. By excluding him, they prevented him from becoming a meaningless high school nobody. They have earned low spots on his hit list because they are hardly worth the bullets it will take to put them down. The bullets Ian intends to use—223 Remington 50 grain jacketed hollow points—might only cost about $0.50 a round, but that adds up quick.

So many questions still need answers. Ian wonders if he should be worried that he hasn't settled on one of the plans yet. That makes the day more exciting, but also nerve-wracking. He enjoys knowing exactly what to do and when to do it. The endgame is fuzzier though because it depends on too many outside factors.

How quickly will the cops be called?

He has a plan to delay the inevitable, but nothing is perfect. His prized possession will only buy him time.

Ski mask or no ski mask?

Wearing the ski mask would improve the odds of him getting away. The cops will probably still figure out it was him, but he can be two states away in a matter of hours if he drives north. On the other hand, a ski mask might rob people of their last glimpse of him. They might die not knowing who saved them from their pathetic lives of mediocrity. That would be sad.

Kill myself? Let the cops do it? Or should I surrender?

Ian isn't sure on the suicide part. How can he fully appreciate his actions if he's dead? The entire world will soon know his name. That's some heady stuff. But the idea of surrendering goes against everything he's trying to accomplish. Maybe if he has the right hostages, he can get away. That would be ideal. Then he could watch the world burn from a safe distance.

What does he want to be remembered as?

Some lame-brain psychiatrist might profile him as depressed or maybe narcissistic, just because he doesn't need their degrees to know he is better than them. They'd try to find a million excuses for what could send a young man to such "desperate measures." They'd look so deep that they forget the obvious.

The fun. The challenge.

Human nature translates to competition in every endeavor. In an absence of true strife, humans find new causes to fight for. Ian considers writing an essay on the subject. That would really give the psych people something to drool over. He deserves a medal for bringing excitement to their tiny town. He's going to put them all on the map.

Once everything is packed, Ian stares at the bags, knowing they will be heavy. He can leave them there or take one bag in today and the other two tomorrow, but he dismisses that idea immediately. He refuses to back down. He should have left more of the clothes at school, but he didn't think about that until now. If the administration conducts a random locker search or does a drill with the local police department, they might accidentally stumble upon his stashes of weapons. He can't take that risk.

Now or never.

Letting himself out of his room, he sneaks down to the kitchen and empties his mom's secret "vacation" fund, the one he isn't supposed to know about. She will blame Thad. Ian only regrets missing that blowout. Just holding a thousand dollars in cash makes him feel invincible. He's surprised to find that much there. His mom goes through cycles where she "borrows" from the fund to fuel her pill addiction then puts it back when she gets paid. Ian doesn't know how she holds down a job.

Maybe she's just a good actress.

He shakes his head to rid his mind of thoughts of her.

This is *his* day.

A noise from upstairs makes him flinch. He needs to hurry, or Little Miss Perfect will be begging him for a ride to school. Inspiration strikes him, and he remembers the nasty taco meat from two weeks ago. Finding a Shoprite bag in the bin of bags to be recycled, Ian wraps the whole container in the bag and seals it as tightly as possible. Next, he grabs one of the packs of hot chocolate mix.

Treasures in hand, Ian dashes back up the stairs, unlocks the door to his room, and retrieves his bags. The weight upon his shoulders gives him a thrill of pride. He feels like he is going off to war, and in a way, it's true. Today, he will war against their stupidity, their apathy, and their whole corrupt system. And he will win. That's the best part. No matter what happens, if he enacts Phase One and Phase Two, the day can be counted as a win for him.

All right, who's ready to die?

Chapter 2:
My Nutters

Monday, 6:15 a.m.
Naomi Harrison-Kensley's Apartment
Emerson, New Jersey

Naomi watches the edges of the bagel gradually become crisper as the toaster does its job. When it springs, she swoops in and grabs the two halves so they don't burn. Waving away the mild pain of touching the piping-hot bagel, she turns her attention to the rest of her morning routine. Lining up the daily pills, she notices one missing. Jogging to the bathroom, she grabs the Claritin-D thinking maybe that will clear her head. She doesn't know if the fuzzy head stems from allergies or a cold. In theory, the potent allergy medicine should work either way, but it would be so much nicer to have definitive answers.

Jack would tell her to take the day off if she doesn't feel good, but despite two years of marriage, he has yet to grasp the colossal amount of work it takes for a teacher to successfully take off for a sick day. Besides, Naomi always feels guilty for making her colleagues cover for her when she can still stand and talk.

The nutters can make it one day without you.

The thought comes complete with Jack's charming British accent.

Yes, but they're my nutters, and they need a little stability in their lives. Naomi silently argues with phantom Jack.

This year, she has two of the three levels of chemistry and a section of biology. She has taught college prep chemistry for the past decade, so that part is second nature to her, but the general chemistry class is new to her. Moody is a mild term for the students in that class. One day, they're engaged in the lesson and reasonably compliant with rules and regulations. The next day, they're pouting and throw teenage tantrums, which usually involves headphones, a phone, and a hoodie pulled up around their ears.

By this point in the year, Naomi knows each student pretty well. Max from period 2 likes to say crazy things to get attention. Randy from the same period regularly loses or breaks pencils. A.J. from period 4 can't get to a class on time if his life depended upon it. Mike Z. from period 6, Jess from period 2, and about half the other kids in Naomi's classes have serious phone addictions. Every spare moment, and quite a few stolen ones, they listen to awful music at ear-shattering volumes. That's not just her old, stodgy imagination. Enough headphone failures have given her the misfortune of listening to the filth first-hand.

Behind the love of f-bomb-dropping rappers, Naomi feels that the students long for a connection with people. They want to feel alive, loved, and appreciated. They don't think adults "get" them, and they think they are the only ones in the world feeling that kind of pain.

Loneliness. Isolation. Inadequacy.

The effort to shield kids from discomfort caused society to inadvertently create a staggering number of crybabies with little to no coping skills. There were two extremes. Either parents got involved so strongly that their child could barely breathe, or they abandoned the kid to navigate life alone. Only a very narrow margin found that happy medium of caring for their kids without doing everything for them.

I love my job.

Some days she believes that more than other days. Jury's still out on what sort of day this would turn out to be. Waking with a headache doesn't exactly give her high hopes, but breakfast and allergy medicine should improve things.

Returning to the kitchen, Naomi places a finger on her bagel to see if it is cool enough to put cream cheese and jelly on. Finding it ready, she doctors her bagel and eats half while retrieving her lunch from the refrigerator. She could take leftover beef kebab from the Mediterranean restaurant down the street, but force of habit made her pack a ham and cheese sandwich. That's okay. She could use the small break from beef kebab. They had ordered in on Friday, and she'd let Jack place the order. That had been a delicious mistake, one that would grant her lunch and dinner for two more days.

She feels the familiar ache of missing him and tries to shake it off. If he'd been home, he wouldn't have been conscious anyway. He'd be in their room snoring like a freight train. If for some bizarre reason he got up early, he'd be sitting at one of the bar stools in their kitchen looking like a scruffy zombie until she took pity on him and gave him coffee.

Missing Jack makes her appreciate having him in her life all the more. She can't imagine life without him. This amuses her because a mere four years ago she'd been perfectly content with being single.

People adapt to whatever situation they're placed in.

Finishing her breakfast, Naomi puts the dishes in the sink and dumps some water on them. She can deal with them officially when she gets home from work. Not that she plans to admit it aloud but washing dishes by hand soothes her. The chore lets her right an obvious wrong and bring order to chaos.

Finding the plastic travel mug right where she'd left it on Friday, Naomi rinses it out, washes it with soap, rinses it again, and dries it with a paper towel. Next, she refills it with pre-made sweet tea. She used to bring coffee to work but had given that up because she wasn't overly fond of lukewarm coffee. The tea tasted fine no matter how long one left it sitting on a desk. Besides, it was kind of nice to have something refreshing awaiting her at the end of a long day.

I need more excitement in my life.

She immediately takes the thought back and squashes it. Excitement is bad. The last "excitement" in her life had been the previous year when her mother went through a few rounds of chemotherapy and succumbed to the cancer anyway. The excitement before that had been her brother's frantic midnight call that Dad was unresponsive and being taken to the hospital.

Thinking of her parents reminds Naomi that she should visit Dad soon. His memory is failing, but he still has more good days than bad ones.

Gathering the school bag that remained untouched since Friday, Naomi lugs everything out to her car. She imagines juggling school stuff, tea, purse, keys, and a baby while navigating two flights of stairs, and then, flattens that thought too. If they want to go the baby route, they need to embark upon it soon, but Naomi isn't sure she wants to take on that responsibility. Some days, she can barely handle keeping herself fed, watered, and adequately clothed. Maybe they should explore the foster child or adoption options again.

Naomi shivers, realizing she forgot her coat. Running back inside, she retrieves the missing coat and pauses to go over the mental checklist.

Stove off. Lights off. Heat off. Lunch transferred to car.

She can't shake the nagging feeling that she's forgotten something but figures it will present itself before too long. Or she'd live without it. Whatever "it" is.

After starting her car, Naomi's eyes fall upon the radio. That reminds her that she never really uses the radio anymore, not since switching her music addiction over to Spotify.

Phone!

The expensive piece of tech sits up in her bedroom smugly absorbing electricity after doing its job of rousing her from sleep. Grunting, she rips the key out and runs back to her apartment. Maybe she should have taken Jack's advice and splurged on that remote starter kit. That way, she could return to a toasty car.

Jogging up the stairs yet again, Naomi wonders if the universe is trying to tell her something like: *go back to bed, you human wreck. Hit the reset button in like an hour.*

Snatching up her phone, she tries to descend gracefully, without waking the rest of the apartment complex. A grumpy noise from inside Mr. Tavish's apartment tells her she is failing at the task, but she doesn't have much sympathy for him. If he can blast rock music on school nights, he can deal with her feet on the stairs in the morning. Pausing at the bottom, Naomi tries to think of another reason she might return to her apartment this morning, just to mess with Amos Tavish, the certified grump.

You're already late.

"Late" was a relative term. Since time was already creeping past when she usually arrived at school, it was indeed late for her, but if she left now, she would still likely beat three quarters of her colleagues to the school. On a Monday morning, that was important because it meant the coveted copy machines would be free for the using.

Her Sunday lesson planning marathon had resulted in quite a few handouts and quizzes that needed copying. Jack sided with the tech guys who wanted them to go paperless, but Naomi and Alycia dared the Chomebook jockeys to devise an adequate way of teaching Chemistry without writing stuff out by hand. If that ever happened, Naomi figures she might just up and quit. Let a new wave of teachers tackle high-tech stuff.

We'll all be holograms someday, but not yet.

If Jack got a promotion or two, they wouldn't really need her salary, but then what would she do? If they said yes to having a baby, the answer would be obvious, but what if they chose to get a few cats instead. Pets of any sort would require some care, but that wouldn't come anywhere close to the time commitment of a full-time teaching job.

These idle musings occupy her during the short drive to work. Pulling in the parking lot, Naomi notes that Ralph and Alycia have both beaten her to the school. That isn't surprising.

Deciding to be spontaneous, Naomi drives out of the parking lot and heads to the nearest Dunkin Donuts. She stops in the parking lot to order a Vanilla Chai tea with the app so she can get the points. The process takes longer than usual because she has to cancel the order twice because it defaults to the one near her apartment instead of the one near work. She adds an extra half-dozen donuts to share and walks in to wait for her order.

Getting into the school building will be interesting, thanks to the unexpected addition of a hot drink. Still, if that's the worst obstacle she faces today, it will be a stellar Monday. The thought of an afternoon meeting puts a slight damper on her mood. She can't even remember what flavor of pain today's meeting will offer. Alycia will know. The woman checks her school email far more thoroughly than Naomi does.

I love my job. I love my nutters. Heck, I am one and Jack knows it.

Chapter 3:
Out of Order

Monday, 7:15 a.m.
Brantford Regional High School
Brantford Township, New Jersey

Luck favors Ian. Arriving at the high school in under ten minutes, he pulls into one of the visitor spots and takes the bags out of his trunk and the back seat of his Jeep. He has two choices: lug everything in at once, which might look a tad suspicious or take two trips. Opting for two trips, he puts the one backpack and the lacrosse bag bearing his AR-15 and some ammunition onto the front passenger seat and locks the vehicle. Then, he picks up the two backpacks, wearing one normally and slinging the other over his left shoulder. The remaining lacrosse bag gets cradled like a baby across his chest.

He should hurry. It's still a little too early for most people to be there, but in about five minutes the number of students entering the high school will change from a trickle to a stream. By 7:30 the first buses will arrive. Everything must be in place by then.

Hurrying through the front door, Ian goes straight to the boys' locker room in the Lower Gym to store the lacrosse bag bearing his most precious cargo. Then, he swings back around to the boys' restroom on the first floor down by the science wing. That normally wouldn't be his first choice, but it's the nearest restroom that offers several stalls. Going to the last stall, he locks himself in and sets the two backpacks down.

Digging out the leftover taco meat, Ian holds his breath and quickly dumps the contents into the toilet. He follows this with half the pack of hot chocolate to further dirty the water. Finding something missing, he uses a few sheets of toilet paper to scrape the sides of the container for more rancid taco juice. He mixes this with a bit of the remaining chocolate powder and smears the concoction on the toilet seat and floor before tossing the used paper into the chunky mess he created in the bowl.

Admiring his work, Ian hangs the backpack from the coat hanger on the back of the stall door. His mind keeps flipping on the issue of marking the stall as Out of Order. He wants to stash weapons in one other restroom. The other candidate restroom already has an Out of Order sign conveniently in place. Unfortunately, it is located far away from the areas Ian intends to work in.

Hopefully, the mess—and the smell—will deter idle people from lingering. On the other hand, he can't make too much of a mess or somebody will call maintenance. That's a risk he must take. If anybody finds his backpack, they will likely just drop it in the main office, but somebody there will search it for identification. He makes sure his previous year's school ID is safely stowed near the top so they won't dig too far.

That got him thinking about the Lost and Found pile. With spring break still looming ahead, the thing will be overflowing. Nobody will disturb the pile today, except maybe to add something. Wrapping one of the loaded handguns in a sweatshirt, Ian zips up the remaining backpack and wanders toward the main office again. He doesn't want the security cameras to sense his hurry.

When he arrives at the Lost and Found table, Ian adds the loaded sweatshirt to the pile then pretends to check a few of the other items. He ends up selecting another sweatshirt from the stack and rearranging things until the one he just added gets pushed near the back-left corner. Taking his new prize with him, Ian returns to his car in time to move it out of the visitor spot. The campus resource officer nods to him and offers a strained smile. Doubtless the man itches to report the parking infraction, but technically, the day hasn't started so Ian is in the clear.

After parking in his assigned spot, Ian dons the new sweatshirt and a baseball cap. Next, he slings the remaining lacrosse bag over his back and picks up the two backpacks by their top handles. Approaching the side door, he kicks it until a sympathetic soul opens it for him. The administration has been uptight about people entering and exiting through the front throughout the day, but they are more understanding outside of normal school hours.

He mumbles thanks but the girl who opened the door for him is already halfway up the stairs to the second floor.

Walking past the special services offices, Ian makes a left down the long hallway toward the Lower Gym. Once again, he concentrates on keeping his walk slow and casual. Sweat on his forehead makes his head itch under the baseball cap. Ignoring the discomfort, Ian presses on toward his goal.

The locker room still bears the lingering haze of steam from the nearby showers. Getting the second lacrosse bag into his locker takes some doing because it is not really made to hold that much stuff. His locker lock should discourage any desperate shoe hunters. Anybody trying to pick up the bags would probably wonder at the weight of them, but generally, kids around here borrow from people they know. Finally, Ian delivers the last spare backpack to the Out of Order stall one floor above the Lower Gym. He doubts he'll get to use the equipment in the backpack, but it's always good to have a backup plan.

His stomach grumbles. Since he has a lot of extra cash on him today, Ian decides to treat himself to a breakfast sandwich. He usually skips school breakfasts, but this is a special day. He decides that bacon, egg, and cheese on a bagel will be an excellent start. A bottle of water and a large coffee round out his meal. The mere thought of the work to be accomplished today gives him a healthy appetite.

Taking the food to an empty table, Ian settles down, sticks in earbuds, and raises the hood of the sweatshirt. Few would bother him anyway, but he doesn't want to spend the effort on a conversation, not when he still has a lot of thinking to do. The routes need to be settled before go-time.

Should I move the timeline up?

Part of him wants to race back to the locker room, grab his AR-15, and get the show going, but that would be a terrible waste. Most of the students haven't even arrived yet. Patience was never a virtue he excelled at, but one could endure almost anything if they knew there would be a better payout later.

Time crawls by while he eats and watches the people around him. The cafeteria noise level still hovers near nothing. Most of the early students are regulars absorbed in finishing homework, playing video games on their phones, eating breakfast, or napping and listening to music.

Ian amuses himself by wondering which of the students around him will be alive at the end of the day. A sense of power fills him. They have no idea what's coming. As the minutes pass, more people file in to wait for the morning bell to send them to their first class. Ian categorizes the people around him as "live," "die," and "don't care." Most people draw the "don't care" label. These people will die so he can make his statement, but Ian doesn't relish their deaths. Very few get the "live" label. These fortunate individuals have each done him a good turn once upon a time.

Malcolm Jones walks by with his shadows, Curtis Ryman and Max Kessler. They don't acknowledge Ian in any way, which suits him fine. If he has his way, they will be dead in a few hours, but he has other priorities to deal with first. Two-thirds of the Trio have history 6th period. That puts them slightly out of his reach unless they pull their usual afternoon stroll. He's counting on that.

Ryman likes Melanie Orlis and Kessler likes Tonya Gilbert. Both girls have chemistry in 106 last block of C days, so the guys are regulars in the science wing. Jones usually meets them somewhere along the way to chat. The only times their schedules get thrown off is if Mr. Wright forces them to take a pop quiz before checking out of class.

Ian tries to remember if they covered any material worthy of a pop quiz. Since he has 8th period and the afternoon runs 8, 9, 6, he should be able to tell if he needs to make an extra trip down to the Glass Lab to deal with some human garbage.

He looks around, trying to spot Little Miss Perfect or her best friend. If he finds one, the other won't be far. When he fails to spot the duo, Ian frowns.

What if she doesn't show up today?
That would ruin his plan.

Chapter 4:
The Hitchhiker

Monday, 7:22 a.m.
Red Rose Avenue
Brantford Township, New Jersey

I hate him. I really, really hate him.

Sherri Colt doesn't mean the words, but she needs something to keep her from freezing to death on the miserable walk to school. Home sweet dump is exactly 1.9 miles from the high school, which is a tenth of a mile short of a free ride on a cozy bus. The cold wind does a stellar job of blocking any warm, fuzzy thoughts concerning her older brother, so she clings to her momentary hatred for the son of a hairless monkey.

What's the point of having an older brother with a heated vehicle if he leaves without you?

Ian occasionally pulls the "I don't feel like attending school today" nonsense, but he very rarely leaves without her because that always gets a lecture from their mother.

A car beeps behind Sherri, making her take an involuntary hop. Landing on a small patch of ice, Sherri throws her arms wide in a desperate attempt to keep standing. It works. It also wrenches her back.

"Sorry!" calls a familiar, cheerful voice. "You look like you could use a ride. Hop on in, stranger."

For an insane moment, Sherri considers limping away, but good sense prevails. Instead, she slowly makes her way over to the cherry red Nissan Altima.

Valerie Marquette pops the door open for her and slides over on the back seat to make some room.

"How'd you end up out there in the cold?" Val wonders. She wears her long, dark hair up in two thick braids today because that is approximately how it will be styled during the play.

"Let her get in first, Val. You can interrogate her after she's warmed up," says Val's mother. Mrs. Marquette is basically everything Sherri wishes her mom would be: kind, attentive, present. She turns back to the driver. "Turn the flashers on and hop out."

"But Mom, I'm allowed one non-family passenger as long as—"

"Don't 'but Mom' me, my car, my rules, sweetheart. Out."

Val's older sister Megan stabs a finger at the button to activate the emergency flashers and unbuckles her seat belt. Muttering about the injustice, she slams the car door and walks around the front to get in on the passenger side.

"She'll get over it," Mrs. Marquette whispers to the girls before exiting the car.

A moment later, everybody gets settled again, and Mrs. Marquette adjusts the seat and mirrors to her liking. She also blasts the heat so some drifts back and warms up Sherri.

"We're going to be late," Megan grumbles.

"It's only 7:25, what definition of late are you working with?" asks Mrs. Marquette.

"They only make a certain number of breakfast sandwiches each morning," Val explains to her mother. She casually reaches over and wraps her hands around the icicles that used to be Sherri's hands. "If you get there after 7:30, your options are cold cereal or burnt toast."

"Well, I can't have my daughters eating such rubbish, can I? Even though I told them both to eat before we left the house. Besides, we have a guest."

"Mom, you're talking to yourself again," says Val.

"Part of my charm, darling," answers Mrs. Marquette.

Checking both directions, Mrs. Marquette executes an illegal U-turn.

"Mom? You know the school's the other way, right?" asks Megan.

"Yes, but the good Dunkin Donuts is this way," says Mrs. Marquette.

Sherri and Val exchange excited looks. Then, Sherri's expression shifts to worry.

I don't have any money.

Following her line of thought, Val leans close to whisper in her ear.

"Mom buys gift cards by the boatload. I'm sure she'll buy you anything you want. You're practically family."

The sentiment puts a lump in Sherri's throat. Her blond hair doesn't exactly blend in with the dark locks shared among all three Marquette women. She flashes her friend a smile, but her stomach churns with unease. There has always been a marked difference between the finances of their families, but Val works hard to make her feel comfortable. She appreciates the effort, but that doesn't make accepting gifts any easier. Sherri can't wait until she is old enough to get a job, then she can treat Val to breakfast for a change.

No wonder Ian works so much.

Aside from keeping him out of the house and away from their mother, the job gives Ian money, which frees him from relying on anybody. He's been working for years. He must have hundreds saved up. Part of her wonders why he never offers to buy her breakfast, and the other half of her shivers at the idea of owing him anything. They'd been a close-knit family long ago, but the divorce and custody battle had kind of drained them of all affection for each other.

The car stops and three doors open, snapping Sherri out of her thoughts. She quickly gets out and joins the others, making sure to check both ways when crossing the section where cars pass from one area of the parking lot to another.

"What do you want?" Val asks. "I'm so hungry I could eat a dozen donuts myself."

"Breakfast sandwich first," calls Val's mother. "I don't want to see any 'I'm so hungry' texts at 9:30."

"9:30's honors physics today," Val assures her mother. "Sane people do not text in Mrs. Meyer's class."

"You know what I mean, missy," says Mrs. Marquette. "I expect you to eat well and hearty here and now." She checks the menu. "Okay, so at least eat hearty," she amends. "Those health options sound awful." She mouths these words toward the girls with her back to the staff, so she doesn't insult them.

"Can we eat here?" asks Megan. She smiles shyly toward the counter.

"Why?" inquires Mrs. Marquette. She drags out the question and follows her daughter's gaze. "Oh, I see. Handsome Face behind the counter must have something to do with this sudden desire to eat in plastic orange chairs. Shall I ask for his phone number when I order?"

Megan avoids her mother's eyes.

"I already have it."

The admission earns a more alert look from Mrs. Marquette.

"Does your father know?"

"There's nothing *to* know," Megan insists. "Matt and I are just friends."

"Mmm. I'll be the judge of that, but for the sake of time, we'll table this conversation for now," says Mrs. Marquette. "Everybody make your selections, please. We have a leisurely eight minutes to eat if we want to avoid the Beast." That was Mrs. Marquette's term for the traffic that magically appears around 7:50 and lasts until 8:10 every morning.

The local police station has an officer there to direct traffic for those twenty minutes, but that doesn't fix the problem. The same thing happens at the end of each school day. Everyone either busts their butt to get there before 7:45 or takes the late and waits it out.

"What do you want, Sherri?" asks Val.

Sherri rubs at the sore spot on her back and checks the menu to see what the cheapest option would be, but before she can order Val closes her eyes and places the back of her right hand on her forehead. Holding out her left hand toward Sherri, she speaks in a horrific imitation of a gypsy woman.

"No, don't tell me. I can sense your desires. They burn from your pretty green eyes."

"Is it too late to pretend we don't know her?" asks Megan. "She's so weird!"

"Uh-huh. I'm gonna blame your father for the dramatic flair." Mrs. Marquette clears her throat and looks at Val and Sherri. "Oh, speaking of drama, do you girls have practice this afternoon?"

"It's a rehearsal," Val corrects, "and yes, we do. Why doth thou make such inane inquiries?"

"Because it means we should order some extra bagels for you to share after school." Mrs. Marquette rolls her eyes at Val's use of Shakespearean language. "And it is not an 'inane' question, but good use of the word."

In the end, they order two medium regular coffees and two medium hot chocolates, a half-dozen donuts, a dozen bagels, and four breakfast sandwiches. Val scarfs down the bacon, egg, and cheese on a croissant, and Sherri has a similar one with sausage instead of bacon.

Mrs. Marquette and Megan both have egg and cheese on English muffins.

Sitting down to eat puts them in a time crunch, but they arrive at the school just ahead of the mad rush. Mrs. Marquette pulls into the little section where visitors park and stops long enough for everybody to pile out. Several thank yous and farewells pass back and forth.

They reach the front door just as the warning bell rings. Exchanging a smile, Sherri and Val dash in opposite directions. Sherri heads for physics, and Val runs up the stairs so she can make it to history. Next, Sherri will have history while Val has honors physics during the second block. Third block, Sherri has choir while Val has band. They will have lunch together, go to theater arts class during the first and second afternoon blocks and finish out the day with English class.

Chapter 5:
Argue on Paper

Monday, 8:00 a.m.
Brantford Regional High School
Brantford Township, New Jersey

Ian walks through the door to English class as the late bell rings. He doesn't want to be late, but he can't quite bring himself to be too early either. Miss Jayne tends to talk to those who arrive first.

"Good morning, Ian," Miss Jayne says in her sing-song, cheerful voice.

He nods coolly. The Pledge of Allegiance spares him from having to respond more definitively.

Too early for that much cheer.

The trek back to his assigned seat passes without incident.

"Good morning, my beautiful people." Miss Jayne's smile brightens even more than usual. She wears a dark purple dress with a long white sweater. Her blond, curly hair falls to her shoulders and bobs every time she nods, which happens frequently. "Please take out a half-sheet of paper."

The class groans. Nothing good ever begins with those words.

"Not again!"

The complaint comes from somewhere in the front row, but Ian misses identifying the speaker because he's digging out a pen and paper. As expected, Cedric asks for a piece of paper, which Ian hands over without comment. The boy stares at the whole sheet, not sure what to do with it. Sighing, Ian gestures for the paper back, folds it in half, creases it, and tears it along the line. The separation isn't perfect, but it works. Handing the slightly jagged piece of paper to Cedric, Ian writes his name in the top right corner of the paper he kept, avoiding eye contact. For some reason, he doesn't want to see the gratitude in Cedric's eyes.

Who will watch out for him after today?

Ian slams the mental door on that question. Cedric has been his shadow since middle school. The Trio had targeted them both. Malcolm Jones especially enjoyed finding ways to accidentally break Cedric's glasses. Ian had once been suspended for shoving Malcolm into one of the cafeteria walls after the third such incident. The principal had been lenient because it was well-known that the Trio had it in for Cedric, but they brushed the behavior aside as youthful mischief.

"We had one last week," protests Douglas Diggs from the seat next to Ian.

"Yes, and you were supposed to read a whole chapter over the weekend," says Miss Jayne. She pierces Doug with a look that says she knows he didn't do the reading. Her smile has a "gotcha" tint to it. "Just a few quick questions, nothing to fear … if you read the book."

Ian can't even give the book's title, so he doesn't bother listening to the questions Miss Jayne poses to the class. Instead, he draws smiley faces and stick figures on his half-sheet of paper. To prevent Miss Jayne from alerting guidance or emailing his mother, Ian writes a note at the bottom saying he'd had a busy weekend at work and didn't get to do the reading.

It won't matter in a few hours anyway.

He longs to write that on the paper, but that would be dumb. His eyes grow heavy, but he resists the urge to nap. He needs to stay out of trouble. He can't afford something stupid like a lunch detention.

After gathering the quizzes, Miss Jayne glances at a few of them and frowns. She sighs deeply then straightens her shoulders and pastes on another smile.

"Clearly that chapter eluded most of us, so let's read parts of it together. It is crucial—"

Ian blocks out the rest of what she has to say.

"I failed that," Cedric says sadly.

"So did I," Ian comments with a casual shrug. "I never do the reading."

"I do," whispers Cedric. "I just don't understand it."

"Something you gentlemen want to add to the conversation up

here?" Miss Jayne's glare demands they pay attention.

Both boys shake their heads. Ian concentrates on getting out his notebook to avoid glaring back. That would draw too much attention.

Satisfied, Miss Jayne calls for volunteers to do some reading. Half the class sinks lower in their chairs while the other half practically springs out of their chairs trying to get a coveted part. Ian waits for the din to die down then politely asks to use the restroom.

"Try to be back in five minutes," says Miss Jayne. It is the same plea as always. Sometimes she has him read a short passage before leaving, but today she just waves toward the door dismissively. She knows he never does the reading, and she also knows he can still pass her essay-based tests.

They have an unspoken deal. He doesn't interrupt too much, and she leaves him alone.

Ian wanders in the general direction of the restroom but pauses for a drink before he gets there. If he spends twenty seconds at the fountain and a minute in the restroom, he will have three and a half minutes to take a walk. He rarely makes it back in the allotted five minutes, but Miss Jayne usually doesn't catch on unless he re-enters at an awkward moment.

The walkabout lets Ian avoid most of the read-aloud portion of class, which he always finds terribly painful. Very few students can read to the class without stumbling over every other word. He returns just as Miss Jayne gives the class a writing prompt for their daily journal entry. Ian enjoys this part because it allows him to do nothing.

"All right, time to set your imaginations free, happy writers," says Miss Jayne. "Today's prompt is this: should the school change its mascot from the broncos to dragons?"

Who cares?

"Of course, we should change, we're not even the right colors to match the Denver Broncos," says Eli Stanfield.

"But we've been the Brantford Broncos for over eighty-five years!" Lily Carter exclaims. "Doesn't that count for anything?"

Miss Jayne raises both hands to silence further debate.

"There are plenty of reasons for both sides. Argue on paper if you please."

Dutifully, Ian takes out his black composition notebook, opens to a clean page, and picks up a pen. If he pretends to write something or actually writes just a few lines, Miss Jayne will be satisfied for the day. She threatens to spot check the notebooks every other week, but in reality, she collects them the last week of every quarter. Ian has enough entries for this quarter to get a passing score, not that anybody will care soon. He almost shakes his head at the pointlessness of everything.

Ian wasn't sure what had prompted the silly idea of changing the school mascot, but the issue has had students and teachers thoroughly divided for weeks. A quick glance around the room reveals seven students wearing some Brantford Bronco apparel. Forest green sweatshirts with tiny horseheads in the upper left corner and even hats, T-Shirts, and sweatpants are everywhere. Kids aren't supposed to wear hats because it messes with the security cameras' ability to identify them, but the administration doesn't fight them too hard on the issue.

They have bigger worries, like whether we should change symbols from an irrelevant animal to a mythical creature.

Ian surprises himself by having an opinion on the matter. Since he has a pen in hand and a blank page in front of him, he decides to participate. It should make time pass quicker anyway.

Keep the mascot the same.

There's history at stake. There's also no real reason to change. Selling more shirts is a piss-poor reason to change your history. This town may not rely on horses any more, but that's not the point.

What is a school mascot or any mascot for that matter? It's a symbol. Something to fight for and wave little flags and get all excited for nothing. The football team's hardly won a game in three years. Changing the stuff on the uniform isn't going to save them.

People suck. They need cheap stuff like this to cling to.

It gives their pathetic lives meaning. Because we all want to be winners. We were promised we were winners. We were lied to.

This isn't about dragons or broncos. It's about control. Make a change. Protest! Pitch a fit. If you whine loud enough, somebody will cave and give you what you want like the freaking baby you are.

The future is yours.

Seize the day.

Be the change you want to see.

And all that rot.

I don't care. If being represented by something that never

existed makes you feel better, go for it.

You want dragons? I'll give you dragons. Hope they burn you.

I'm done with you.

Ian draws a little dragon next to the entry then rips it out, crumples it up, and shoves it in his pocket.

Miss Jayne raises a questioning eyebrow but lets it go.

Ian spends the rest of class drawing dragons in his journal. Whole scenes come to life. Small stick figures wave branches at each other. One shakes a sword at a dragon and gets his head bitten off. Another stabs a dragon's foot before being crushed underneath that same foot. A third tries to ride the dragon and gets squished between its two wings. Yet another gets thrown into a wall.

At 9:01, the bell releases Ian from his furious scribbling.

Chapter 6:
Sad Story

Test day, my favorite. Until it comes time to grade them.

The first few minutes of class pass in a flurry of last-minute questions that make Naomi doubt some of her students even bothered studying for the test. Since the test is designed to take about forty minutes, she indulges their questions before handing out the paper. It takes another half-minute for them to settle into their test-taking mode. Luckily, period 4 is a tiny class this year. It's nice to have a break when it comes to the number of tests to grade.

Once certain that nobody needs her this second, Naomi wanders to the back door that enters the chemistry prep room to greet her colleague. They hadn't had a chance to catch up much since their morning free time had been spent either making copies or providing extra help to the last-minute crammers.

She finds Alycia frowning down at her phone at the desk right next to the printer.

"Hey, what's that expression for?" Naomi wonders. "Monday can't be that bad already, can it?"

"There's been another school shooting," says Alycia. "Maryland this time. Two injured. One dead. Kid marched in before school even began, shot a girl he knew then killed himself when confronted by a guidance counselor." She holds up her phone to show Naomi the article.

"That's sad, and becoming too common a tale," comments Naomi. "Who's the second injury?"

Alycia shrugs.

"The guidance counselor, I think."

"Glad it wasn't any worse," says Naomi, though she knows that three families have been shattered today.

Peter raises his hand, so Naomi goes over and has just about the same conversation they have every test.

"I don't know how to do this?" says Peter, jabbing a finger at one of the questions.

"What do I always tell you to start with?" queries Naomi.

"The given," mumbles Peter.

Naomi starts to walk away.

"But am I on the right track?" asks Peter.

"I can't answer that." Naomi walks to the far side of the room and takes a position where she can see most of the students working.

"Okay, I didn't want to do this, but you've given me no choice." Peter reaches into his pocket and pulls out a dollar bill.

The rest of the class giggles.

Naomi sighs and rolls her eyes.

"Put your money away and take the test, Peter. You're distracting other people."

"Yeah, if I fail because of you, I'll kill you," calls Andrew.

Peter throws down his pen.

"Guidance! I need to go to guidance. That's a threat." He starts to get up.

"By all means," says Naomi, waving to the door. "I'll call ahead and let them know you're coming."

"No, that's okay," Peter replies, resuming his seat.

"Good. Then, take the test." Once the Peter affair is under control, Naomi flings a disapproving look at Andrew who smiles and ducks his head. "Andrew." She fills the name with a warning. "You can't say things like that, especially in the day and age we live in. Use your good sense."

"Sorry," says Andrew.

Things settle down after that until students start finishing the test. For some reason, most don't understand that some people need longer to take a test than others. Letting them listen to music when they're done helps, but as soon as they sit next to one of their friends, they start talking. Naomi has her hands full just trying to keep them reasonably quiet so the slower, more methodical students can finish up the test.

When the last exam is collected and squirreled away in the to-grade folder, Naomi glances at the clock. With only four minutes left in class, she decides not to fight the children to do anything productive. Instead, she packs up and goes back to the corner by the prep room. She stays in the room to make sure nothing crazy happens.

Like clockwork, at one minute before the bell rings, the students get up and congregate by the door.

"Step away from the door," calls Naomi. "Seriously people, find seats of some sort."

Peter, of course, hops up onto the lab counter.

"Except there," Naomi amends. "You can't sit on the lab counters. Bench, yes, counter, no."

She spends the next minute arguing with Peter over why there would be such a silly rule as no sitting on counter tops. The bell rings, ending the debate. Naomi gratefully steps into the prep room.

"That kid is exhausting," she mutters.

"Which one?" asks Alycia. "No, wait. Let me guess. Peter."

"How'd you know?" Naomi asks, despite knowing exactly how. The kid's name pops up every class for something stupid he's said or done.

"What'd he do this time?" wonders Alycia.

"Offered me a whole dollar for test help," Naomi responds with a wry smile.

"You should have taken it and used it for the burning money demo," says Alycia.

"I'll consider that next time." Naomi squeezes past the chair Alycia occupies and dumps her stuff on her desk.

The prep room might not boast a lot of space but it offers a peaceful place to hide from the world on one's off hours.

"How'd they do on their quiz?" Naomi asks, seeing the neat stack of completed papers next to Alycia.

"Some good, some terrible." Alycia shrugs. "The usual. I swear I taught them this stuff, but you wouldn't know it by some of their answers."

"Anything as interesting as 'chicken,' 'bagel,' 'French fries,' or 'Jesus' this time?" Naomi inquires. She's digging deep in her memory banks for some of the weirdo answers she's gotten.

"Mostly 'IDKs' or big, fat blanks," laments Alycia. "I hate blanks. They hurt my soul." She gestures to the top paper where a neat little "-13" decorates the second question.

"Ouch. Yeah, blanks hurt," comments Naomi.

"Do they realize they're killing me slowly?" queries Alycia. She stands and gathers some papers she wants to take with her.

"If the announcement doesn't show up on their phones, probably not," says Naomi.

"Cynic."

"Realist," Naomi corrects.

"See ya later," says Alycia.

Naomi waves and eyes the gigantic mess that has taken over her desk. Somehow first block came and went without any progress being made on that front.

That's a problem for later me.

Chapter 7:
Choices

Not wanting to suffer through an academic study hall, Ian checks himself into the Nurse's office. Mrs. Finigan greets him wearily. He's a regular, but since it's a Monday and the study hall is relatively early, she understands he probably doesn't have much work to make up. Both cots are unoccupied too, which helps. If somebody comes in who truly needs the bed, Ian will miraculously recover from his headache.

He tries to nap, but his mind refuses to rest. Plans and fragments of plans swirl in his head. The hard thinking gives him a real headache.

Once again, he considers the primary targets: Little Miss Perfect, the Trio, and his ex-girlfriend. Liana always looked down on him. She never took their relationship seriously, but he would have done anything for her. It might be cliché, but if she can't stand by Ian through some rough times, then she doesn't deserve to live.

Sheridan, Little Miss Perfect, represents everything that went wrong in his family. Mom had been normal pre-Sherri. Post-Sherri Mom couldn't handle her depression without some serious prescription drugs. That makes Sherri a sizable part of the problem. Besides, killing her serves the double purpose of punishing Mom for being a lousy mother.

The Trio pushes everybody around or ignores them.

33

Ian wants to spread the misery evenly. If he can take out the Trio, he gets seniors. Little Miss Perfect covers the freshmen, and Liana checks off the sophomores. There aren't any juniors who have done Ian particular harm, so he thinks back over his countless walkabouts.

6th period is the last of the day. If Ian begins upstairs with Little Miss Perfect and company, the nearby rooms will have an Italian class, another English class, and a Spanish class. Both might have a handful of juniors, but they're not strictly speaking, junior level courses.

Going after Liana first will put him dead-center in the science wing. Since juniors take biology, that would provide him with a few convenient junior-rich environments. It's an option. The order would run sophomores, juniors, freshmen, then seniors.

Targeting the Trio first runs the risk of not letting him reach any of the other primary targets, which is completely unacceptable. Ian really wants to take them out, but not at the expense of making his larger statement. Unfortunately, no day features a schedule where all five primary targets have class in adjacent rooms.

"Would you like some water?" asks Mrs. Finigan.

It takes a second for Ian to realize she's addressing him.

"No thanks," he answers. "I'm good."

"Okay. Well, let me know if you change your mind," she says, heading back into the office part of the suite of rooms set aside for the school nurses.

Ian returns to his musings.

If he's fast, he should be able to reach two target rooms before a lockdown is called, but only if he starts with Liana or two-thirds of the Trio. Little Miss Perfect's class is upstairs. Liana's classroom is located almost at the center of the school on the first floor, and the Glass Lab where two-thirds of the Trio will be is right smack dab in the center of the school, near Liana's classroom. He plays both scenarios in his head multiple times. Going for Liana followed by Sherri means a lot of backtracking if he expects to reach the Trio. Logically, that means he ought to start with the two-thirds Trio, but he must begin with Sherri if he wants to go in order of priority.

The lacrosse bag with the AR-15 should carry him through one classroom, but he'll have to reload after that. Instinct should have people scrambling to get away from him as soon as he opens fire, but any time he needs to stop and reload, he'll be vulnerable. Even extended magazines only hold thirty rounds. He has a few handguns to protect himself while reloading. Bullets aren't perfect. He expects to spend three to four bullets per target. He's gotten good at headshots in several first-person shooter games, but real guns are much heavier and harder to aim with any sort of accuracy. Given the nearness of his targets, Ian doesn't need to be terribly accurate, but he must be quick.

If he can duct tape some magazines under his sweatshirt, that might speed up the reloading process. Each backpack and the lacrosse bag all have sizable rolls of duct tape, but Ian hasn't tested the strength of the tape on clothes. If the tape fails, either by sticking too well and fouling up his ability to reload or dropping the magazine at a terrible time, the whole plan could collapse. Digging the magazines out of the lacrosse bag or one of the backpacks would take longer but run less risk of losing the ability to reload altogether.

Do I have enough ammo?

Ian doesn't like second guessing himself, especially now when it's far too late to do anything about it. Both remaining backpacks—the one left in the science wing men's restroom and the one he has with him—have four magazines for the three Glock 19s he brought. The original plan would have seen the last gun in the bathroom up by the remaining one-third Trio, but Ian had stuffed it in the sweatshirt on the Lost and Found table. He put the backpack where planned, but not the gun itself. Each Glock 19 set him back about $500, but he is comforted by the ability to keep weapons in multiple locations. His precious AR-15 cost him twice that, but today, it will earn its keep in full. Surprisingly, the spare magazines for the semi-automatic rifle only cost about $15 a pop. Ian can only hope he gets to use every magazine he brought with him.

What if I chicken out?

Ian hates the thought, but he is forced to consider the possibility. He's fired the weapons many times before. Looking older than his age helped in that regard. Still, he's never killed anybody, except in his dreams.

To distract himself from the horrible thought of failure, Ian uses his phone to check out some recent news headlines. The one that catches his eye concerns a botched school shooting. He quickly skims the article and silently vows not to make the same mistakes. The kid should have confirmed the kill he wanted before checking out.

Don't worry, man. After today, nobody's going to remember your failure. Promise.

Chapter 8:
The Great Water Bottle Hunt

Monday, 9:30 a.m.
Brantford Regional High School
Brantford Township, New Jersey

Sherri Colt tries to listen to her history teacher's lecture on the Russian Revolution, but Mr. Vance is practically old enough to have been there and well-practiced in the art of rambling. She doesn't need to glance around to know her classmates wear glassy-eyed expressions.

Toby is absent. That explains the lack of entertainment because he's not around to say stupid things or get into trouble by doing something dumb just to see what kind of reaction he can get from Mr. Vance.

Sherri's mind wanders to the mini-play she's producing and performing in with Val. They know their lines but they're seriously running out of time to gather the necessary supplies. The actual performance in front of a live audience won't take place for another two weeks, but the graded performance takes place tomorrow, which is why they get a double period rehearsal today. The week of the mini-plays will be awful and glorious. Sherri can almost taste the excitement and sleep deprivation. This is only her second performance with The Wild Horse Players, the freshman theater group. They drew the plays at random. At first, she wasn't thrilled with getting *Princess Melia's Plight*, but the more she read the script, the more she looked forward to the challenge of bringing it to life.

Midway through rehearsing some blocking late in the skit, Sherri feels every eye fall upon her and snaps her attention back to the moment. Mr. Vance is looking at her expectantly. Panic twists her stomach into a knot. It's not the first time he's caught her thinking of anything but history.

A glance at the clock tells her she might have an out. Instead of asking him to repeat the question, she swings her right hand up and asks to use the restroom. Rolling his eyes, Mr. Vance mumbles an affirmative and waves her toward the door.

Escaping as quickly as possible, Sherri takes three rapid steps away from the closing door before pulling out her phone and texting Val.

Meet me sci br.

She heads down the hall toward the nearest stairwell at a fast clip. The science hallway is located down in the low 100's while her history class is in the mid 200's. Normally, she'd take her time, but not when she wants to meet Val.

Pushing through the door to the girls' room in the science wing, Sherri mentally kicks herself for not bringing her water bottle to fill on the way back. She stops suddenly, mid-step, not sure where her water bottle is.

"Somebody put a giant glue trap down or what?" asks Val.

"I lost my water bottle," Sherri answers, consciously returning to a normal standing position.

"Where did you last see it?" Val inquires patiently.

It's a familiar conversation to them since Sherri misplaces her water bottle two to three times a week.

Thinking hard, Sherri recalls having it in physics during the first block, but can't remember any other details after that.

"I had it in physics," Sherri reports. "After that, it could be anywhere." She shrugs helplessly.

"Let's check the Lost and Found first," says Val, grabbing Sherri's left hand and tugging toward the door. "It's been there the last two times it walked off."

Sherri considers resisting and actually using the facilities, but she doesn't have to go at the moment. Besides, it will give her an excuse to leave third block if necessary.

"I've got to get a leash for that thing," Sherri mutters, pushing back through the door to the girls' room.

They turn left down the hallway toward the main office. A long table in front of the glass windows contains a wide variety of abandoned clothes and random items. The office assistants try to move non-clothes items to a box inside where they'll be somewhat better protected, but a wide variety of things still end up on the Lost and Found table.

Running a practiced eye over the table, Sherri sees the usual selection of sweatshirts, jackets, sweatpants, and T-Shirts.

"It's not here," she notes sadly.

"What are you two doing out here?" demands a familiar voice.

Spinning right, Sherri gapes at her older brother. He hardly ever speaks to her anymore. She's become accustomed to "sullen and withdrawn" Ian. The version standing before her practically quakes with anger. He's also pale and sweaty. She can tell by the damp rings near the armpits of his dark blue T-Shirt.

"Are you all right?" she asks instinctively. "Ian?"

"Get back to class," Ian orders, brushing past her. He reaches around her, plucks up one of the sweatshirts from the far left corner, and zips down the hall away from them.

"Your brother kind of scares me sometimes," Val whispers, once he's a few rooms away.

"Me too," Sherri murmurs, watching Ian turn the corner toward the library and media center. A phantom feeling washes over her, making her stomach flutter. She's seen Ian in some dark moods, but she's never seen his eyes quite like that, angry and accusing for no good reason.

"I should get back or Mrs. Meyer will yell," says Val. "She doesn't like when I leave class for more than two minutes. I don't even know how she keeps track."

Sherri nods and escorts her friend back to room 100 where Val has honors physics then continues down the hallway until she reaches the double doors to the staircase up. She ought to be hurrying back too, but her thoughts linger on the memory of Ian's weird expression. She can't remember the last time they had a nice conversation.

Tears sting her eyes, but she pushes them away with a wave of anger. Ian can't upset her. She won't let him. The silent pep talk works to some extent, but Sherri's heart aches with unbidden memories of Old Ian. Her brother wasn't always a jerk. Once upon a time, he was her horsey and knight in ill-fitting plastic armor. He had carried her up trees on his back and worked with Dad to teach her how to ride a bike. Their parents' divorce had changed him.

Truth be told, the divorce had changed her too, but instead of driving her into a shell, it had brought her out. She'd sought refuge in school and by doing as many activities as she could. Dad had been in an overly generous mood during the custody battle. He'd paid for everything from club soccer to horseback riding lessons with Val. That only lasted until Dad lost visiting rights because of a couple of drunk driving and reckless endangerment incidents. Things had spiraled out of control from there until finally, Dad overdosed on prescription meds last year. Those had been dark days, but she'd had Val through it all.

What can I do to help Ian move on?

Last year, during Ian's brief relationship with Liana Ackerman, Sherri had seen glimpses of Old Ian, the goofy kid who likes to make people laugh.

He needs a girlfriend … or at least a good friend.

Sherri arrives back at her history classroom before reaching any conclusions, giving her plenty to ponder during the rest of the block. Then, only choir stands between her and lunch. The thought of lunch triggers a low rumble in her stomach. That's followed swiftly by another gut-wrenching shot of anxiety at not having a lunch. Val won't let her starve, but Sherri hates relying on others, even her best friend. The situation sends her mood spiraling, and it's all she can do to keep her head up the rest of class.

Chapter 9:
A Thousand Ways to Die

Monday, 10:40 a.m.
Brantford Regional High School
Brantford Township, New Jersey

Ian sits in the back of Mrs. Harrison-Kensley's 1st period General Chemistry class and plays on his phone. She and Doc G. let him get away with it because he's already finished the two worksheets they set out for the class to complete. He just has to pay enough attention that he can answer the occasional question posed to him. It's an unspoken deal they reached after two months of hellish battles of will. Doc wasn't happy about the arrangement, but she came around. After all, she's got enough problems keeping the other kids in line and on task. Some days, the class resembles a circus more than others. Today is actually a fairly low-energy day for most of Ian's peers.

HK's a decent teacher, a tad on the stuffy side, but nice enough. She always lets kids use the restroom upon request, though she does give dirty looks if you ask two or three times in the same class period. If she has time, she even sends an email home informing your parents of the time you spent out of class. Luckily for Ian, his mother rarely checks her email. HK's pretty chill about nurse passes too. Teachers aren't really allowed to keep kids from going to the nurse, but Ian already used the nurse card this morning. He might ask to go there in a little bit just for the walk, but Mrs. Finigan is going to kick him out or call his mom or something stupid like that. She's told him before "off the record" that she doesn't want him back twice in one day unless he's bleeding or throwing up.

He plays *A Thousand Ways to Die* on his phone and listens to the class with half an ear. Some days his classmates amuse him, but more often than not, they just annoy him. As his assigned seat's dead center of the back row, he's literally surrounded by idiots. Thus, he's gotten very good at blocking out their inane chatter. He should have just passed the class last year when he had the chance, but it's too late for such regrets now.

In the game, some fool comes at him with a chainsaw. On the campaign side, Ian tried the chainsaw and admits that the kill effect is cool, but only noobs try melee weapons in battle royale mode, especially when the opponent has a loaded shotgun. The game makers tried to even out the power of the various weapons, but Ian has logged enough hours to earn several mods that speed up reload time and how quickly one can switch weapons. He wastes the guy and switches over to a handgun to deal with three opportunists coming at him from another side.

His screen flashes red, telling him that he's taking fire. The strobe-like effect says that the fire is coming from multiple directions. Diving behind a pillar, he checks left first, switching to sniper mode instinctively. Once he zooms twice, he places the crosshairs between his opponent's eyes and fires a round. The game pauses and follows the path of the bullet until it crashes into the other player's head and explodes in a round of pixelated blood.

HEADSHOT!

Ian's coin total shoots up by 1000, but he doesn't have time to bask in the glory. There are still eight players polluting his board. He's muted the sound so he can listen to music at the same time, but when he turns back to the pillar, he can see little chips flying off of it, indicating that it's under fire. He quickly reloads even though he's only used one of the seven bullets this gun holds.

Crouching low on the left side, Ian again turns to sniper mode, but this time, he sticks to 1x zoom so he gets a slightly wider field of view. He spots the enemy sniper a split-second before the rifle swings his way. Switching to 2x zoom, he fires, resets, and fires again.

CONFIRMED KILL

The coin count goes up by 100. That's disappointing, but nothing to worry about. The match clock reads 2:31. Ian is running out of time. Every player will forfeit all coins earned if there's not a clear winner in two and a half minutes. Ian has scored two headshots this round. He doesn't want to lose that much gold.

Deciding to take a risk, he toggles to inventory and chooses an Omniscient Bush. The special item costs 2000 gold crowns and tells the player where every enemy soldier is hiding. The downside is that the bush appears with the player who planted it in a random spot on the level, usually in the center where everybody has an easy shot at the person. To balance this, the player who planted the Omniscient Bush gets thirty seconds of immunity.

Ian gets lucky. The Omniscient Bush teleports him to the center as expected, but he finds most of his foes almost instantly. Four of the eight remaining enemy combatants have hidden out in the Old Abandoned Shack. Choosing a grenade launcher, Ian lobs four frag grenades, one for each window that lights up red.

His gold count rises by 400.

He's used five seconds.

Arrows pointing bottom left, bottom right, right, and bottom show Ian which direction he can find his enemies. The guy directly behind him is charging with a pocket knife, the one weapon excused from the thirty second immunity. Growling low, Ian wastes four seconds using the grenade launcher to fend off the stupid pocket knife, clobbering the guy wielding the knife, and using the baby bayonet on the front to skewer him.

He earns 150 gold for the melee kill.

He has 21 seconds of immunity remaining. Eight seconds vanish while he orients himself, turning to face the three remaining threats. One guy is perched high in a tree, patiently waiting for the chance to end Ian. He'll be easy pickings. The second remaining enemy is in a foxhole in WWI gear, hunkered down behind a machine gun. He's probably the biggest threat. The position of the third and last enemy isn't immediately apparent. That means either he's using a special item to combat the Omniscient Bush reveal or he's being a sore loser and running for the map edge. If he steps out, the round will end automatically. Ian will receive the victor's bounty, but every player will be penalized for poor sportsmanship. The penalty fee is 500 gold crowns. Ian can afford it, but he doesn't want the game to end that way.

With 11 seconds remaining, Ian lobs a few frag grenades at the guy in the foxhole. He sees a hail of bullets waiting for his immunity to end. If he misses, he's toast. Without waiting to see the results of his shots, Ian switches to sniper mode and offs the guy in the tree.

6 seconds remain.

Quickly checking his items, Ian scrolls through his options. The first useful item he comes across costs 5000 gold. He hesitates, but chooses it anyway.

The move prompts a short video clip. The view zeroes in on Ian's last foe. The camera view swings out and around as a large hand descends from the sky and smashes the guy into the earth.

HAND OF GOD!!!

Ian's gold count goes up by 250.

CHAMPION!

The gold count jumps by 2500.

The scroll bar at the bottom explodes with comments. Most are random symbols indicating curses. Ian put the child filter on just because it amuses him to watch his opponents rant with substitute curses.

That was awesome.

A fair amount of comments say similar things. Ian thanks his fans and taps a few keys until the bow emoji pops up.

Pumping a fist in victory, Ian lets out a whoop and leaps out of his seat.

"Did you win?" asks HK. Her steady tone indicates only mild curiosity.

"Oh, yeah!" Ian confirms. "Wiped out all those losers!"

"Bet you cheated," says Ricard Samson, glaring at Ian.

"He used 'Hand of God,'" reports Simon Kessler.

"That's not cheating!" Ian declares.

Rolling her eyes, HK throws out her hands like a mage casting a spell.

"Boys! There will be no bickering in class. Least of all because of a video game. Got that?" HK takes a few seconds to stare down Ian, Ricard, and Simon. Then, she draws a deep breath. "There are only twenty-ish minutes of class left, so if you can just hold down your crazy for a while, we can get through the rest of the lesson. Okay? Ian, please play quietly. Ricard, focus. Simon, put the phone away. You don't have phone privileges until we're done here."

The rest of the class passes almost peacefully for Ian. Since he doesn't feel like diving into the stress of another battle royale, he plays on campaign mode, choosing a medieval map and a flail. He's not very good with the hand to hand combat in the game, so he dies in short order. Switching over to a modern desert map, he goes back to his specialty, the sniper rifle. He finds it relaxing to scan for targets, zoom in, line up the shot, and send the bullets on their merry way. By the time the bell rings, he's racked up ten kills with two being headshots. The gold payout for campaign kills is much less than the live battles, but Ian likes going for the achievements too.

Chapter 10:
Lucky Lady

Monday, 11:24 a.m.
Brantford Regional High School
Brantford Township, New Jersey

Naomi checks the clock far across the cafeteria. The evil thing still says 11:24. She'd brought one of the donuts with her, but that had lasted all of two minutes tops. She glares at the clock before letting her gaze wander around the crowded room. Directly in front of her camps a table of freshmen boys. They're like puppy dogs with scraps of meat. With one hand a skinny kid smashed between two bulkier friends jealously guards his lunch. With the other, this same child torments a nearby neighbor by poking him in the side and stealing fries. Naomi rarely intervenes, deciding to let the harmless nonsense slide, but when another boy snatches up a half-eaten apple and raises it to throw at the fry thief, she steps forward, catches his eye, and shakes her head. He smiles brightly and lowers his arm, giving the apple a small toss and taking another bite to reinforce the air of innocence. She settles back to her primary occupation of holding up the cafeteria walls for an hour.

Time does its usual café-duty crawl.

Five minutes later, to relieve some of the tedium, Naomi takes a stroll around her zone. Tables 11-22 have the usual collection of cliques divided primarily by gender and sports teams. The tables farthest from Naomi feature junior girls, gamers, and the freshman misfits to her left, middle, and right respectively. In front of them sits another two tables

45

of junior girls and a table of junior boys. The middle row holds sophomore boys straight across. The row closest to her is mainly freshmen boys but many have left or are about to leave for the gym, which thankfully stays open during the hour-long lunch period.

There is no reason on Earth they need this long for lunch.

Naomi appreciates having an hour to eat, relax, and prep, but she's been around long enough to know that the students need about twenty minutes to eat. The rest of the time gets spent watching videos or playing games on their phones, taking silly and stupid videos of each other, and copying homework from one another. Back in the day—different school, different lifetime—Naomi had to eat in twenty-five minutes and so did the students. And they all survived.

Lost in thought, she nearly runs into a colleague.

"Sorry," she says, stopping abruptly.

"No worries," Jason Mefton assures her. "I know a café-duty zombie when I see one. Do you get to leave now?"

"Nope, this is my once-per-cycle, hour-long tour of duty," Naomi says.

"Lucky lady." Jason shifts a step right to give her some wall space. "Pull up a wall. Tell me about it."

"'Lucky' is not exactly the term I'd use, but at least it happens on a fairly light day." Naomi checks that the wall is clear of ketchup before turning and leaning against it. "What are you in for? I've had this duty all year. Where's Sutton?"

"I'm in for life—or the end of the year, whichever comes first," Jason jokes. "Sutton wanted some quality extra help time with her low-level kids. He-who-has-a-higher-paycheck-than-I agreed and did some magic duty shuffles. One minute, I'm on hall duty and then BOOM, conscripted."

"Bummer." Naomi tries to summon a sympathetic smile for the man.

"Eh, there are worse fates," Jason notes philosophically. "Like restroom monitor." He shrugs his shoulders in a mock shudder. "Erik was telling me he found rancid meat in the science hallway boys' room this morning."

"Gross. Who would do such a thing and why?" For not the first time, Naomi wonders what exactly goes through kids' heads sometimes.

"We may never know," says Jason. "But I'm going to avoid that restroom for the rest of the day. Erik called it in but the maintenance guys are busy trying to prep for the big snowstorm we're supposed to get Thursday."

"Do you think it'll come?" Naomi inquires.

"Maybe. It's a little early to be checking the snow day calculator, but I'll keep you posted as we get closer," Jason promises. He pulls out his phone and checks a weather app. "There's still a snowflake on Thursday, but that could change."

"Do you want it to come?" Naomi can't tell much from his tone of voice, but the young teacher is pretty much bouncing on the balls of his feet.

Oh, to be twenty-something again.

Not that Naomi has a say in the matter, but she would much rather have a snow day later. They just had one last week. At this rate, they might even have to give back some spring break days. That would be awful.

"Sure! It might give me a chance to catch up on my grading." Jason gestures to a large stack of papers lying on the abandoned table in front of them. The pile lies dangerously close to a puddle of blue liquid, most likely Gatorade. "Tests, quizzes, labs, you name it, I've probably given it in the last few days. I didn't get a chance to work on it this weekend because I got tickets to a Knicks game. They lost but it was still awesome."

Naomi nods to acknowledge the statement since there's really no need for a response. The kid will continue talking with or without further input from her. She mentally shrugs. He's a nice enough kid, and besides, listening to his chatter helps pass the time.

Undaunted by silence, Jason launches into a detailed description of the basketball game he'd attended Friday. Once finished, he moves on to Saturday activities. He'd spent most of the day at a party for a friend turning twenty-one.

"I don't remember much of Sunday," Jason admits cheerfully. "Had a massive headache, but it was worth it."

Internal alarm bells ring inside Naomi's head. She should probably stop the kid from talking before he says something stupid. She doubts any of the self-absorbed students are listening close enough to decipher his meaning, but the fact that he doesn't realize such a conversation shouldn't happen on school grounds is worrisome.

"I wonder if the pizza's any good today," Naomi muses. It's a graceless transition but Jason doesn't seem to mind.

"It should be," says Jason. "I think it came from Joey's today. When do you get to eat?"

"Next period." Naomi glances at the clock. "Eleven and a half minutes, but who's counting?"

"Nice. I have to wait until the second afternoon block. Got to deal with period 8 first," Jason laments. "But they're going to start on a digital learning playlist, so it shouldn't be too bad. What's the rest of your day look like?"

"Lunch, prep, and period 6," Naomi reports. She winces.

"What's that face for?" asks Jason. "That sounds like a nice schedule."

"My prep period won't be much of a prep today," says Naomi. "I have to do the book inventory for three levels of chemistry."

"Ouch. Why three levels?" Jason's brows knit together, indicating his confusion. "I thought you only taught two levels of chem."

"I do," confirms Naomi, "but I cut a deal to get out of doing the ordering for our department."

"Sounds like you got the heavier end of that deal," Jason comments.

"It's all right. I had some students haul them to the back room already," Naomi says with a shrug. "The prep room's a bit tight at the moment, but I'll ask Alycia's 6th period to help haul them back when I'm done."

"Child labor, eh?" Jason's brown eyes twinkle as he says it.

"Exactly."

"Good luck with that." Jason's tone speaks of doubt.

Naomi just smiles.

You'd be amazed what kids will do for scratch-and-sniff stickers.

She really should have done the inventory last week or the week before, but more appealing necessary tasks kept cropping up. Since they'd received a polite but curt email over the weekend dictating that it must be done by Wednesday, she figures she has put the task off long enough.

Finally, the bell rings and sets her free. Bidding Jason farewell, Naomi heads to the women's room to wash her hands before lunch.

Chapter 11:
Fire Hazard

Monday, 12:15 p.m.
Brantford Regional High School
Brantford Township, New Jersey

Despite what she told Jason, Naomi feels kind of guilty for putting off the book inventory for so long. Picking up her lunch from the teachers' cafeteria refrigerator, she pauses long enough to microwave the ham and cheese sandwich for fifteen seconds, just enough to take the chill out of it.

"Set your stuff down. Take a load off." The cheery invitation comes from Corrie Kelman. The biology teacher sits alone at the center table, penned in between a stack of stuff to grade, a few textbooks, and a Chromebook.

"Can't today." Naomi's two-word answer is filled with regret.

"Where are you off to?" asks Corrie.

"Hot date with the book inventory," Naomi replies.

"Ooohh, sounds like fun," says Corrie, wincing sympathetically. "I just did them Friday."

"Yeah, right up there with root canals and paying taxes." Naomi checks the temperature of the ham to see if it's perfect. Finding it a tad on the cold side, she sticks it back in the microwave for another ten seconds.

"I thought you had off 9th period too?" Corrie's tone turns it into a question.

"I do," Naomi admits, "but this could very well take me two periods." She shrugs. "Who knows. I may be here after school too. Working through lunch is just a bid to cut down on after school hours."

"That makes sense. Text me if you need help later. This is my easy afternoon. I remember that task being a bear." Corrie eyes the stack of papers near her right elbow. "Just give me an hour to deal with some of this mess. Then, I can come help."

"I appreciate the offer, but I think we'd need a crowbar to squeeze you into the back room with me," says Naomi. Finally satisfied with the sandwich temperature, Naomi gathers up the rest of her lunch and heads for the door. Before swinging the door open, she pauses long enough to finish her explanation. "On the optimistic off-chance that I can make serious headway, I had the kids move all three book collections to the back. Things are a serious fire hazard. Wish me luck."

"Good luck!" Corrie calls.

Throwing quick thanks over her shoulder, Naomi weaves her way through the lunch tables, which now host collections of gloomy-looking eighth graders waiting for study hall to end so they can eat.

How do they not starve?

The question has no answer. Naomi nods to the study hall teacher on her way past. She can't remember the man's name, but he's an English teacher who happens to be a doppelganger for the band director. He returns the greeting then flicks his gaze back to scanning the eighth graders. The dull look to his eyes reminds Naomi of Jason's statement about "café-duty zombies."

He might have a point.

The trip back to the overcrowded prep room proceeds without event. Reluctant to get crumbs on the textbooks, Naomi practically inhales her sandwich, chasing it down with generous chugs of sweet tea. She weighs the merits of munching on her pretzels with getting a head start. Deciding to use the pretzels as motivation, she sets the clear plastic bag atop a haphazard stack of paper randomness in plain sight. This will be her first goal. She promises herself the bag of pretzels as soon as the college prep chemistry textbooks are logged.

Casting a baleful glance at the nearest stack, Naomi wiggles her fingers to loosen them before setting her hands over the keyboard and tapping out her login information. It takes her three times because the computer has clear issues with letting her in, but finally, she's in. Seconds later, she has opened the correct google form. Many lines of data stare back at her, daring her to touch them.

Picking up the nearest book, Naomi examines it for its condition, makes a few mental notes, and then locates it on the document. She places an "x" in the box marking the book present and updates the condition notes. There's no significant change in this book, thank goodness.

She whips through seven more books with no drastic changes before running across one with a brand new pen drawing of a particular piece of the male anatomy. Rolling her eyes, Naomi double-checks the page it's on. Noticing that it's just the title page, she rummages through her bag until she finds a pair of scissors and surgically removes the offending page. Next, she updates the book's condition note to "title page removed because it was defaced."

Midway through the battle, Naomi stops to organize the books. She moves a stack of ones she's looked at to her left and replaces it with a new stack. Slowly, piles grow on her left and shrink on her right. Eventually, she needs to shuffle them around and utilize the back and side tables to safely host the books. Having witnessed Alycia's four-month ankle twisting saga the previous year, she does not want to be explaining a concussion to the school nurse or filling out the worker's compensation paperwork.

Minutes crawl by while Naomi leafs through every single one of the hundred and sixty-something red General Chemistry textbooks. Just as the bell rings to end 8th period, Naomi puts the finishing touches on the first of her three lists. As mentally promised, she rewards herself with a lovely bag of salty goodness and more sweet tea. Needing to prolong the break, she next visits the restroom since she didn't actually stop there before when she washed up for lunch.

Within ten minutes, she's back to work with a new stack of books, white ones this time. This list goes faster for two reasons: there are less books and they're pretty much brand new since the lower level general chemistry class is new to the district. It also helps that these books have never gone home with students, so the only chance they get to deface them is in class and they're usually too busy with their phones to bother anymore.

Score one point for phone obsessions. Less time to draw obscene images on textbooks.

The third and final list takes her right down to two minutes before the last class of the day. Naomi spends these two minutes neatening the stacks. She'll press her 6th period students into service if they're in the mood. Typically, all students are up for any sort of work that doesn't involve normal school stuff. Carrying books around qualifies. If they're not in the mood, she might still get one trip out of them before having to beg Alycia's students.

As the bell rings ending 9th period, Naomi realizes she still needs to gather the materials for the demonstration she wants to run. Praying they don't burn down the room before she can make it to class, she scrambles to get the vacuum pump, hoses, and a fresh pack of marshmallow peeps ready to go.

Chapter 12:
Prop Problem

"This is going to rock! I'll get the glitter and—"

"No." Sherri Colt's flat tone deflates some of her best friend's enthusiasm.

"Why not?" Valerie Marquette's pouty expression gives her the definite air of a put-out princess. "Glitter's awesome!"

"Awesome," Sherri agrees, "and expensive and messy and just, no." She ticks off the items on her fingers as she goes. "This is a five-minute skit, not Broadway, and besides, Mrs. R. will have our heads for chew toys if we screw up the stage this close to an actual performance."

With a dramatic groan, Val collapses into the chair next to Sherri and throws an arm across her forehead.

"But how can we accurately portray Princess Melia's plight if we can't use Draygor's most potent weapon against her?" she inquires. A flash of inspiration blazes to life behind Val's eyes. "Oooohhhh, oohh, ooohhhh!" She emphasizes each noise with little slapping gestures in Sherri's direction.

"Speak before you explode," Sherri orders, smacking Val's hand aside before it can gouge out one of her eyes.

"What about silver sequins?" A maniacal grin consumes Val's face. "With the right lighting, it could give the same effect as glitter."

"This project's due tomorrow," Sherri reminds her friend. "Where are we going to get sequins for an entire shroud or have the time to sew them into place?"

"That's the best part!" Val's exclamation draws several dirty looks from nearby groups but she forges on undeterred. "I have just the thing!"

Sherri quirks an eyebrow, daring Val to make a point.

"Two years ago Megan was a mermaid for Halloween, remember?" asks Val.

"I don't think your sister's going to let you butcher her award-winning costume," Sherri says, trying to gently break reality to Val. Internally, she admits the mermaid costume would solve their prop problem. It must boast a few thousand silver sequins.

"I won't butcher it," Val protests. "Much," she adds in response to Sherri's doubtful look. "Besides, Megan hasn't worn it since that day. She has no use for it. I'll simply explain … to Megan and Mom … how much we need it to pass our theater class."

Sherri tries to imagine a world where such a plea would matter to a sibling. Her brother, Ian, would probably just slam a door in her face if she got that far into a conversation with him.

"What?" Sherri wonders, failing to follow Val's logic due to errant thoughts of Ian.

If possible, the grin Val wears turns a shade eviler.

"Mom won't let us fail," Val promises. Whipping out her phone, she zips off a lengthy text message to her mother. A long minute passes while Val checks her phone every three seconds to see if her mother replied yet.

Sherri watches Val's expression change as the return message is finally received, read, and comprehended. The contortions Val's face goes through are quite impressive. They include relief, triumph, dismay, and finally, urgency.

Without explaining, Val leaps out of the seat and bolts for the stage stairs, nearly flattening Avery McDougal on the way.

Curious, Sherri scrambles out of the theater chair and races after her friend. She arrives just as Val and Avery both lay hands on a large cardboard box, reach in, and pluck out a shiny, silver mass.

"Mine!" says Avery.

"Hands off," Val growls at the same moment.

"Ladies, what is going on over here?" Mrs. Reese's voice sails high with the question.

"I need this!" The declaration comes from Avery and Val simultaneously.

"Give me the costume," orders Mrs. Reese. Once she has it safely folded over her crossed arms, she stares down both Avery and Val. "Now, one at a time, explain what you need the silver mermaid costume for."

Silence answers her as the two girls eye each other sullenly.

"Avery," Mrs. Reese prompts.

"I need it to make a magic unicorn," explains Avery.

"And you, Val?" inquires Mrs. Reese. "What is it to you?"

"We wanted to make it the glitter shroud that traps Princess Melia in the Shadowlands." Val sounds almost embarrassed.

"Can't it be both?" Sherri flinches, surprised by her own question.

Mrs. Reese glances back at Sherri with an intrigued, *do-tell* expression.

"Um, I mean if we don't destroy it, it might fit both skits," Sherri says.

"But I go right before you," Avery complains. "There's no way I'll be able to change that quickly to let you use it."

"That won't be a problem," Mrs. Reese assures Avery.

"But Mrs. R. how can you—"

Mrs. Reese cuts the girl off with a small, delicate wave.

"Teacher here," she says.

Avery, Val, and Sherri share baffled glances.

With a sigh, Mrs. R. continues her explanation.

"The costume should be pretty easy to repurpose from Avery's use in *The Magic Unicorn* to Val's use in *Princess Melia's Plight*. I'll just have to adjust the schedule a bit." She turns to Avery. "How long do you need to change?"

"Five minutes," Avery mumbles.

"Great. Then you can go after *The Summoner's Handbook*, which is four skits before Val and Sherri," announces Mrs. Reese. "Will that satisfy everybody?"

The girls agree and silently watch as their teacher slips off stage right, taking the shroud/unicorn costume with her.

Avery's shoulders droop slightly.

"Yeah, I know the feeling," comments Val.

"What feeling?" Sherri queries.

"I kind of wanted a rousing fight." Avery shoots her a wry smile.

Reaching into the cardboard box that had recently held the silver sequined mermaid costume, Val draws out two wooden swords.

"Don't know if they'll be any good for your skit, but they'll serve this purpose," says Val, tossing a sword to Avery.

"Hey, where's my weapon?" Sherri levels a mock glare at her friend.

"You don't get one," Val replies.

"Why not?" Sherri's tone teeters on actual offense.

"Because you're the princess," answers Val.

"Which one?" Sherri fires the question suspiciously.

"Melia, of course." Val's tone implies that it's a dumb question.

"Ah, that's okay then," says Sherri, relaxing.

"Why is that okay?" Avery asks tentatively.

It's Sherri's turn to indulge in an evil grin.

"Because Melia is a shape-shifting dragon princess and she can fry both of you sorry sword-wielders in a heartbeat."

Nearly in perfect sync, Avery and Val drop into guard positions, swords at the ready.

Mrs. Reese breaks up the playful fight soon enough so the girls can return to prepping their individual plays during the next block. Sometime between first block and lunch, Sherri had completely forgotten that they had received special permission to miss other classes for rehearsals.

"To be continued," Sherri says, bowing to Avery and Val.

"You're staying next block right?" Val asks Avery.

"Yeah, Mr. Penn looked like he ate a bad apple when he signed the permission form, but he signed it," says Avery.

"Excellent, then we'll finish this last ten minutes of class," Val promises.

"I look forward to it." Avery gives them each a sly smile then saunters off to find her play partner.

Chapter 13:
Beautiful, Tragic Day

Monday, 1:27 p.m.
Brantford Regional High School
Brantford Township, New Jersey

"Colt! Finally living up to your name, I see," calls Mr. Bello. "Great! Keep it up!"

The urge to slow down tempts Ian, but his legs fail to cooperate. Most of his peers are engaged in a pathetic game of kickball. Several girls walk the outer circuit of the track. Tony Salinger jogs slow loops. Ian's the only one running full-tilt. He's already lapped Salinger twice. Sweat pours off Ian in rivers. He needs to move to silence the doubts and fears clamoring in his head.

You'll lose your nerve.

Coward.

Loser.

You'll get caught.

You'll wind up dead.

What do you hope to accomplish?

You're just like the rest.

I'm nothing like the rest!

Ian barely refrains from shouting that last thought. For a while he empties his mind by concentrating on the pain. It's been forever since he put forth this much physical effort into anything, let alone gym class. His body protests the sudden physical activity. He's spent hours in his room and on the range lifting his AR-15 to a ready position but running didn't make it very high up on his priority list for preparations.

That might be a mistake, but it's too late to fix now.

He spends the next few laps at a slightly slower pace, giving himself a pep talk.

You can do this. You'll be remembered forever. You can immortalize your name, but only if it's spectacular. Fail at this and you'll be just another loser who lost his nerve.

These and similar thoughts move through Ian's head in an endless cycle. By the time he reaches the cool-down lap, his thoughts return to his intended targets. He'll never get away with it if he kills his sister first, but he finds it fitting that she leave this world as the center of attention. Most of him doesn't really want to fully "get away with it" anyway. If she's the first to die and he's the last, it will stamp the incident start to finish with the Colt name.

Living carries its own brand of horror. The cops and psychologists will spend so much time pouring over his motivations that they'll lose sight of his accomplishment. He'll have to overshoot because odds are good that some of the victims will live through the initial onslaught. Still, he only has to reach 18 confirmed kills to be the most infamous high school shooter in the United States. No matter what they say about him, as long as he can kill 18 people, they will have to give him his due and remember him.

Adam Lanza killed his mother, 26 more people at Sandy Hook Elementary School, and then himself, but he can keep the kiddie club record. Ian doesn't plan to go after an elementary school. Same for colleges. The dude who went after Virginia Tech got 33 confirmed kills, and he can keep the college record. Ian wants the high school record.

I can do this. Should I aim for the heart or the head?

Anything else will leave too much up to chance. Ian refuses to be one of the losers near the end of the Wikipedia list who only end up killing one or two people and wounding another dozen. Nobody remembers the wounded. It just opens the way for disgruntled idiots to file lawsuits.

Can't sue the dead.

If he wants to have his name top the list altogether he'd have to best the Islamic terrorists who took out a school in Beslan, Russia, but Ian has no delusions about competing with terrorist groups. His goals are far more modest. He mentally pits himself against the single-shooter icons, and unlike most of those guys, he has a good plan. He's not going in amidst a haze of blind rage.

Tough, but doable.

"All right, that's a wrap, people," shouts Bello. "Bring it in!"

The call makes Ian flinch.

Panic grips him.

I'm not ready!

A chilly breeze calms him.

It's a lovely, late winter day, much like September 11, 2001 was a nice fall day. Of course, Ian doesn't remember any of that, but he's heard his mom rambling about that "beautiful, tragic day" on enough anniversaries. Usually, it's with a glass of wine in one hand and a pill bottle in the other. Her father died in one of the towers. Ian's been dragged to the memorial at Ground Zero enough times to picture every part of the haunting place.

The sun blazes brightly in the sky, bringing more cheer than warmth, but it's a start. The idea of people whispering this date forever sends a thrill through him. He stops moving, closes his eyes, turns his head toward the sun and absorbs the rays of light like a heavenly blessing upon what he's about to do.

Without opening his eyes, he pictures the stadium seats filled to overflowing with mourners. If he strains hard enough, he can almost hear their cries and read their signs and slogans. He's going to move this town like nothing in it's boring history ever has.

"Colt! Hurry up!" Bello stands at the side entrance holding the door open for him. "You'll be late for class."

Can't be late.

Ian allows himself a small smile as he jogs toward the school.

Chapter 14:
Phase One: First Kill

Monday, 1:58 p.m.
Brantford Regional High School
Brantford Township, New Jersey

They say the first kill is the hardest, but Ian knows Mr. Kellen's schedule. The man prides himself on never keeping to a predictable schedule, which is mostly true, but he usually opts for a late lunch if he's in the high school. On any given day, the district's security consultant could be doing a spot-check on the middle school or one of the eight elementary schools, but not today.

Exiting the Lower Gym after hastily changing, Ian nearly runs into the man.

"Sorry!"

"Hey, Ian. Running late again, are we?" asks Keith Kellen, nimbly sidestepping to avoid a collision. A large coffee occupies one hand while the other clutches a white, grease-stained bag.

"Yes, sir," says Ian, grateful Kellen's hands are filled.

"Better hustle then. Maybe Miles will let it slide this time." Kellen shuffles sideways a step before turning to continue down the hallway.

"Hopefully," Ian comments, adjusting his grip on the heavy lacrosse bag. After a three-count, he calls after the security consultant. "Oh, I almost forgot. There's something you should see in the equipment locker."

Kellen pauses mid-step to consider Ian's words.

"This isn't a lame attempt to get a pass from me, is it?" he inquires.

"Nope," Ian replies.

"Can it wait until after school?" asks Kellen.

"Don't think so," says Ian. Backing through the door he just emerged from, Ian starts walking toward the equipment locker.

Please follow. Please follow.

Each step into the busy gym makes Ian's palms sweat more, but he quickens his pace, practically running the last few paces.

The door slams shut behind him.

Moving to the back left corner, Ian sets down the lacrosse bag, kneels, unzips the side pocket and withdraws one of his handguns.

"What is it?" wonders Kellen, stepping up behind Ian.

Spinning to face the man makes Ian so lightheaded he nearly misses, but it's impossible since only two feet of space separates them.

The shot strikes Kellen high in the chest causing the big man to stumble back a step before collapsing. The coffee cup and white bag plummet to the ground. The impact dislodges the lid, sending scalding coffee all over Kellen's legs and Ian's shoes. He feels the heat of it sink through the laces holes and cloth tongue. The food bag unfurls, hurling a wave of greasy air upwards.

For several seconds, Ian can only stare at Kellen. A small, neat hole decorates the man's chest. It leaks blood but not as much as Ian thought it would.

His hands shake so badly he nearly drops the gun.

Hot bile turns his throat raw. Clearing his throat turns into a coughing fit which brings tears to his eyes.

"Get a grip!" he growls, wiping his palms on his shirt one at a time. His eyes stay on the body several seconds before darting to the door. Mastering his emotions, Ian spits toward the clear space next to the body.

He shakes himself and really looks at Kellen again.

Another three seconds pass before he realizes the man's still breathing.

Moving closer, Ian meets Keith Kellen's shocked gaze. The man's face is twisted in pain. His mouth moves like he wants to speak, but no sound will come.

Ian's senses swing way past hyper-alert. Individual beads of sweat on Kellen's face appear crystal clear to him. The stench of raw fear and desperation—mostly sweat, blood, and burnt coffee—fills the air.

No turning back.

Leveling the gun at the man's face, Ian finishes the job.

The second shot rings through his skull like a drill.

He freezes and waits. His heart pounds so hard he can hardly concentrate well enough to listen. The gym classes might already be on their way out to the field, but there's still a chance that a lingering teacher heard the shots.

His breaths come in shallow gasps and he's so lightheaded, he could faint any second.

Doesn't matter if anybody heard. Get moving!

Tucking the handgun into his waistband, Ian pulls his sweatshirt low over the weapon. He considers taking a moment to reload the handgun, but if he stops now, he might lose his nerve. Pulling a crumpled baseball cap from the sweatshirt's front pocket, Ian yanks it into place. Then, he retrieves the lacrosse bag from the ground and steps gingerly over the body.

A crunch draws Ian's attention downward. His right foot has caught the corner of the takeout bag holding Kellen's lunch. The cheerful visage of a freckle-faced girl stares back at Ian.

The irrational need to dig in and eat whatever the bag holds wars with Ian's churning stomach. He's so disoriented that he almost leaves the Lower Gym altogether without enacting the best part of his plan.

Drawing a slow breath, Ian steels his nerves and heads into the boys' locker room.

One down, seventeen to go.

Chapter 15:
Phase Two: Primary Target

Monday, 2:02 p.m.
Brantford Regional High School
Brantford Township, New Jersey

Ian gazes at his most prized possession. The bulky black box looks like an alien creature with its many antennae sticking up in perfect order. Flipping the "on" switch kind of disappoints him. It's anticlimactic. After waiting two seconds to feel a sense of exhilaration or power, he snatches up the lacrosse bag stuffed with guns and ammunition.

The pamphlet with the cell phone jammer said it should be able to block Wi-Fi connections too. That should buy him time, but it's also going to alert people to trouble very soon.

Exiting the Lower Gym at a sprint, Ian turns left and heads toward the cafeteria. He makes a quick right down the hallway toward the technology offices, the media center, and the computer lab. Upon reaching the end of that hallway, he turns left and crashes through the doors leading upstairs. At the top, he barrels through more doors and turns right.

Sherri's English class is held in room 204, which lies midway down this hall on the left side.

Ian pauses outside the room. The view through the glass shows Mr. Buckle writing something on the whiteboard at the front. Dropping to his knees, Ian unzips the bag and checks that the AR-15 is ready to go. The thrill he's been waiting for crashes down upon him, causing his shaking arms to tremble even more.

Another three seconds tick by while Ian quiets his mind. He can't go into this next phase panicked. He needs to be cool, calm, and collected.

Lifting the gun out, Ian cradles the weapon, stands, and gently kicks the bag to his left so it will be easily accessible as he moves on.

He's forced to lift the gun up with one hand so he can swing the door open, but it's back in a two-handed grip before the door finishes granting him access to the room filled with freshmen.

Striding in, Ian scans the room, searching for his primary target.

The room abruptly goes silent.

Most eyes swivel in his direction. He feels the heat and intensity of their attention and despises them. The expressions of strangers get locked in a state of confusion. But he doesn't care about them.

Each passing second is its own tension-filled eternity.

Finally, he spots Little Miss Perfect and her sidekick sitting directly in the center of everything. Sherri's head pops up and their eyes lock. Surprise, recognition, and confusion pass over her face in rapid succession.

Lifting the gun to his shoulder, Ian peers through the scope. His sister's white shirt fills the view. As only about ten feet separates him from the target-rich zone, the scope is more of a hindrance than a help. He lifts his head clear and moves his finger to the trigger.

The weapon comes alive in his hands, spitting out bullets as fast as he can pull the trigger. The first rounds sail toward his primary target. A pencil holder in front of her explodes along with that ridiculous action figure she carries around. He waits only long enough to see the first few bullets strike her before sweeping the weapon right toward her sidekick.

The students in the rows in front of the pair scream with fright and pain as the AR-15 rounds strike flesh and bone.

The steady chatter of the weapon churns in Ian's ear, deafening him to the wave of screams rising from the students.

Most freeze in their seats. Some fall out of their chairs and cower. Others are flung out of their seats and slump to the floor.

Movement to Ian's right catches his attention as the AR-15 clicks harmlessly.

Ian reaches for another magazine before remembering that he forgot to take them out of the bag.

Mr. Buckle is almost upon Ian, charging like a bull.

Leaping backwards, Ian instinctively whips the rifle up under the man's chin. He didn't have a great starting angle, but the metal barrel still connects with the man's chin, forcing him to stumble backwards.

Holding the rifle in his left hand, Ian pulls a handgun from the hiding place at his waist and shoots the English teacher from point blank range.

The man collapses.

Ian looks to the remaining students. Each face wears an expression of pure terror. Everybody who can move is pressed into the corners as far from him as possible. Several bodies litter the floor.

Thinking quickly, Ian fires several times into both corners before turning and sprinting for the lacrosse bag he left by the door.

How could you be so stupid?

The question stems from his frustration over forgetting to carry several magazines with him.

He lands hard on his knees beside the bag, ejects the spent magazine, reaches for a fresh one, and slams it home. Quickly, he shoves the rest into the front pouch of his sweatshirt. It creates an awkward bump, making it look like he suddenly sprang a beer belly, but he can't worry about the fashion statement.

Where do I go next?

A gasp to his right makes up his mind for him. Leaping up, Ian turns the gun on the woman staring at him open-mouthed. The first three shots barely miss her head as she ducks into the classroom. In her haste, she hip-checks the door jamb on the way in, dislodging the magnet. Before Ian can reach the door, the woman slams it shut.

He races over and glares in through the glass. Their eyes meet, and their faces are mere inches apart, separated by a thin pane of glass. Ian jiggles the door handle even though he knows it's useless. The teacher backpedals as fast as she can.

Ian's mind races.

Rage sweeps over his whole body. Rearing back, he slams the stock of his rifle through the glass window and sweeps the remaining shards clear.

The teacher is on the far side of the room shouting something to her students.

Ian raises the gun.

The woman wisely drops down behind her desk, taking the phone with her.

Soon every speaker in the school crackles to life.

Ian freezes, shaking with helpless anger.

"Attention. Lock the school down. This is not a drill. Lockdown! I repeat: enter a lockdown! Lockdown!"

Reaching through the broken glass, Ian scrapes his right arm reaching for the door handle. Swinging the door open requires him to step back, but soon, he's through and able to enact his revenge.

He does so with a fresh hail of bullets.

Chapter 16:
Chaos

Monday, 2:04 p.m.
Brantford Regional High School
Brantford Township, New Jersey

Fresh off a rousing fantasy fight, Sherri Colt and Valerie Marquette arrive late to their English class. Mrs. Reese had refused to write them a pass even as she made them clean up their props, gather their scripts, and straighten the set pieces that had fallen victim to the epic battle. Everything works out fine though because they slip into the room just as Mr. Buckle begins taking attendance. You're on time in his class as long as you can be butt-in-chair before he calls your name.

Sherri slides into her seat as he reaches her name.

"Present!" she chirps.

"Close, Colt. Very close," says Mr. Buckle with a friendly nod. He continues calling out the names of other students.

Most students answer promptly, but occasionally, one has to be prodded into verbalizing his or her answer.

Sherri spends the rest of roll call unpacking and preparing her desk. First, she places the wooden pencil case she'd made in shop class last semester on the top right side of her desk and artfully arranges a handful of writing implements to her liking. Next, she places a small orange dragon figure named Tiberius next to the pencil case. Catching Val's eye, Sherri points to the dragon and bobs her eyebrows, earning a scowl and an exasperated headshake from her friend.

"Take out your composition books and start your daily journals," instructs Mr. Buckle. "You have ten minutes. I'll set a timer."

After digging around in her backpack, Sherri comes up with four almost identical composition notebooks. She'd tried to color code them but many boring hours in previous classes have rendered most of them pure black or blue at this point, depending on which pen was in range at the time. She pulls them forward, props them on her desk and shuffles them to read their titles. As her fingers brush the right one, she senses a huge shift in the mood.

The class goes silent. Not just quiet. Silent.

Aside from major test days, that's unheard of.

Looking up, Sherri immediately notices a figure standing in the front of the room, right next to Mr. Buckle's stolen music stand. He's wearing jeans, a forest green hooded school sweatshirt, and a Broncos baseball cap.

And holding a gun.

A really big gun.

Sherri's eyes move past the weapon to the figure's face. The shock explodes within her at the same moment the gun swings toward her and starts firing deafening chunks of misery and pain.

Instinctively, she clutches the notebooks to her chest and stands up.

They do little good as four points of pain ignite in Sherri's gut almost at once. The bullets propel her backward, flinging her across Jorge Hernandez's desk.

Screams rise around her.

More pain radiates from her left arm. Just before she loses consciousness, Sherri sees Val crumple in her seat, a bright red stain spreading across her white Wild Horse Players T-Shirt.

Chapter 17:
Lousy Connection

Monday, 2:05 p.m.
Brantford Regional High School
Brantford Township, New Jersey

"Hello? Hello?" Naomi Harrison-Kensley takes her phone away from her ear and looks at it. The icons stare back at her innocently. "Guess I'll talk to you later," she murmurs. Dropped calls with her husband when he is overseas aren't terribly rare, but she'd been fairly impressed with the connection this time, until it cut out completely.

Normally, she would be in 6th period, but she'd completely forgotten about the life skills class trip scheduled for today. She'd prepared a demo and everything. Upon finding only one student waiting for her, Naomi sent the kid to the media center and bid her co-teacher farewell for the day before bolting back to the prep room to call Jack. Even a short conversation with him was better than nothing.

Shrugging, Naomi taps over to her contacts list and finds the number for her hair salon. She's long overdue for a cut and color, and she rarely gets a bonus period off. Pressing the call button, she raises the phone to her ear and waits. When several seconds tick by without the customary ringing, she checks the phone's connection bars. To her surprise, she has zero bars. The school doesn't have the greatest reception at the best of times, but she's never had a problem placing calls before.

Weird.

Mentally shrugging, Naomi scrolls through her apps until she finds Triple M, which stands for Murder, Mayhem, and Madness. It's a silly find-the-hidden-objects game centered around various crimes. The first screen pops up just fine, but when she tries to log in, she gets the wait-for-it wheel followed by a polite message to check her connection.

Weirder.

If this keeps up, she'll have no choice but to do something productive. That would be disappointing. A quick check of settings reveals no Wi-Fi connection. As she tries to decide if her phone simply hates her, Naomi notices that the volume has risen noticeably from 106. Curiosity draws her over to the door separating the prep room from the classroom in question.

She immediately spots several horrified students staring down at their phones.

One kid near the door frowns down at his device and mutters a few curses.

Deciding to investigate further, Naomi opens the door and peeks in to get a better look. About three quarters of the students look visibly annoyed. The remaining quarter stare at their peers in confusion.

"Grademaster's down," Alycia announces from the front.

"Everything's down!" cries a boy sitting in the last row.

"How do you know that?" inquires Alycia. "Aren't you supposed to be working on your warm-up?"

"I was just getting into it, but my tunes cut out," says the boy.

"Did that break your hand or just your head?" asks a girl sitting to the boy's left.

"Shut up," snaps the boy.

A dozen conversations break out around the room.

"You'd think it was the end of the world," Naomi notes as Alycia comes over to chat.

"Hard to imagine life before the Internet," Alycia agrees. "We'll be back to smoke signals soon."

"It's just the school's crappy network," claims Nate. "They'll reset it soon."

Naomi knows his name because he voices an opinion on everything and has since the first day of school.

"I can't look up the answers to the warm-up," complains Erica.

Alycia rolls her eyes and shoots Naomi a *kill-me-if-you-love-me* look.

"There's this wonderful thing called a textbook," Alycia tells Erica. "It works just like the Internet, but it has physical pages to turn."

Erica sighs but gets up and goes toward the back, stopping short while still in the middle of the room.

"They're gone," Erica announces.

Naomi follows her gaze to the barren back shelves.

"Whoops. Hang on," says Naomi. "I have them." She slips back into the prep room to retrieve an armful of books. She dumps them on the back lab counter before plucking up the top one and walking it over to Erica.

"If you need a textbook, they're in the prep room!" Alycia calls to her students. "The answer's also in the notes we took Friday. Assuming we took notes Friday. We did, right?"

A handful of students get up and retrieve textbooks. Grumbling, the class slowly adjusts to temporary life in an Internet-less dystopia. A few settle back into work with headphones plugged in, using playlists already downloaded to their phones. The rest get to work with grumpy expressions fixed in place. Life returns to a normal Monday afternoon, third block state of being.

"What type of meeting do we have today?" Naomi inquires, surprised she hasn't had a chance to ask before now. She considers looking it up on her phone before remembering that the option doesn't exist for her currently. She winces, not quite ready to admit that she's almost as addicted to her phone as the students.

"Department," Alycia answers. "Don't you remember the three-page agenda Dalton sent through yesterday?"

"I don't remember much that woman sends us." Naomi snaps her fingers in mock disappointment. "And darn, can't even look it up now that the Internet's down. Guess I'll just have to go take a nap." The idea has merit once she voices it.

"Have fun," Alycia says.

"I shall," Naomi replies.

Retreating to the prep room, she moves to close the door again but thinks better of it.

"If anybody else needs a textbook, they're the first stack here," she tells her colleague.

"They should be all right, but thanks," says Alycia.

Grateful to have a winter coat at the ready, Naomi returns to her desk, pulls her coat into place, and selects a playlist that doesn't require a Wi-Fi connection. Turning the volume down so that she can barely hear the soft music, Naomi fluffs the coat as she would a pillow, closes her eyes, and lays her head down. There's always a stack of grading that she could be working on, but the afternoon meeting might require energy and patience to get through.

A series of faint pops sound in the distance. Idly, Naomi's brain puzzles out what could make such noises. Loud bangs or the sound of an imminent ceiling collapse could be easily explained as the English or social studies classes above them rearranging the furniture. Sudden, staccato pops and explosions could also mean Nikki's present next door wowing her class with cool demos, but the AP chemistry teacher doesn't have a class this period and had a professional development thing scheduled for today anyway. For one rare moment, 104 lies unoccupied.

After a slight pause, a second string of faint popping noises sound. These are different, slower and more deliberate than the first. Naomi's mind automatically likens the noises to firecrackers, but that can't be right. Shaking her head and shifting position, she taps the side of her phone until the volume raises a hair. Soothing music fills the air around her desk.

A beep indicates that an announcement will soon take place, but the defective speakers in the back don't carry the actual message. Naomi prepares to ignore it, but dead silence suddenly falls next door. A shaky voice says something unintelligible to Naomi, but something has definitely changed. Forcing herself up, she races to the prep room door in time to catch the tail end of the announcement.

"—down! I repeat: enter a lockdown! Lockdown!"

The speaker cuts off but not before a string of rapid-fire pops, frantic screams, and incoherent shouts come through the open line.

Every eye fixes on the speaker box for a tense second.

Naomi catches Alycia's eyes and sees a mirror image of the emotions flooding her: fear, disbelief, doubt, and determination.

If this is a drill she's going to have some choice words for the administration.

Nobody moves.

Then, everybody moves.

"Into the back!" Alycia shouts to her students.

The words snap Naomi out of the dazed state.

104's wide open.

Whirling, she stumbles back through the prep room door headed for the other connecting room at a dead sprint.

Chapter 18:
Shields

Her boots slip on the smooth floor tiles, forcing Naomi to grab hold of a desk so she can redirect her momentum. Upon reaching the door, she whips it open and rips off the magnet then grabs the outside handle to confirm that it's locked.

It's not.

The handle swings down freely, causing her soul to run cold. Dustin Capernack, the physics teacher who's been having trouble this year, must be absent again. Sometimes the office people give the substitute teachers a key, but mostly, they unlock the door for them for convenience. Nikki would normally fix the door lock situation, but today, she might not have stopped by the room on her way to the curriculum writing professional development thing.

If this were last year, Naomi would simply lock it herself, but she doesn't have a key this year. Knowing what happened gives her very little comfort. Her mind scrambles for a solution as she plucks off the clips to lower the blinds. She has to jump to reach the last one because the Chromebook cart is in her way. After banging her knee on the bulky metal beast, inspiration strikes her.

The cart!

Scrambling around the cart, Naomi flicks up both locks with her

73

toes, wrestles the unwieldy thing into position, and stamps down on the locks again. It's not perfect, but it's better than nothing. She considers moving a bunch of lab stools in the way, but she's beyond out of time.

She still has to deal with the window shades along the back of the room. That task takes another minute. Then, racing back to the prep room, Naomi darts inside, shuts the door firmly, and leans back against it. She's torn between leaving it open a crack to listen for announcements and keeping it shut. The fact that 104's door is unlocked weighs heavily upon her. She only hopes they'll all live long enough to miss any announcements.

The prep room's a wreck, but thankfully, they only need to worry about Alycia's class. Naomi can't imagine trying to stuff two classes of twenty-plus students back here, especially with the bulk of their textbook collection present.

Unlike a normal drill, the kids are completely silent, staring at the two teachers with wide eyes.

Alycia pulls Naomi aside, turning both their backs to the students.

"What's wrong?" The question's low but still loud in the strained silence.

"The door's not locked," Naomi says. She grimaces as Alycia's grip on her arm tightens.

A girl within hearing range whimpers and starts hyperventilating.

We need to give them something to do.

Naomi's eyes fall upon the textbooks.

"The books," Alycia whispers, coming to the same conclusion.

Quickly, the pair directs each student to grab a textbook and hand it forward. Each book arriving on the left goes to Alycia who adds it to the stack already blocking half that side. A few get handed to Naomi on the right, but since there are vastly more books on the left, that side fills up first. Alycia then joins the book brigade by handing off the excess books to Naomi. Soon, both sides are nearly completely blocked.

"Everybody grab a book, especially if you're near the front," Naomi instructs.

"Sit down if you can, and get as far back as you can," Alycia adds.

The student mass shuffles and shifts. Several students cram themselves back under the desks.

Shoving the skeleton out of the way, Alycia grips the nearby table and maneuvers it in front of the left path, providing one more barrier.

The sight of Vern, the skeleton, gives Naomi another idea. It's too late to fumble through keys to find which one locks the prep room doors. But they can still block them. Wedging another few textbooks under Vern's wheels, Naomi places the skeleton in front of the prep room door to 106.

For 104, she yanks two textbooks off the top of the stack and mentally apologizes to them. Then, she opens them and wedges them by the door. In theory, if the door tries to swing open, it will hit a mass of paper and stop.

"Get behind the barrier," Naomi says to Alycia.

"No way. There are two doors," Alycia points out.

"Two doors, but only one's open," Naomi argues.

A muffled bang tells them somebody's fighting the Chromebook cart.

That sorts their disagreement quickly. Together, they wrestle the nearest stack of books up to the prep room door leading to 104. Winded, they do the same for another stack and hunker down next to the makeshift barrier.

More banging noises cause Naomi's heart to rattle around inside her.

The banging stops, and Naomi realizes things have turned much worse. Instinctively, she moves as far back into the corner next to the door as she can. Alycia is on the door's right side, inching as close to the stack of books in front of the students as she can. She's practically wedged under the sink by this time. She waves for Naomi to cross the short gap and join her.

Naomi shakes her head, ducks, and shuts her eyes, pulling her knees up to her chest. Her mind goes eerily blank.

Father God, protect us. Don't let us lose one of these kids. Not one.

Gunfire rips through the door and textbooks, sending chunks of paper and wood flying.

There's a brief pause.

The screams get lost in the bone-rattling chatter of rapid gunfire.

The door starts to slide open, making a mess of the book left as a sentinel.

Naomi tries to push the door closed but she has a terrible angle and no leverage.

The muzzle of a very large gun pokes through the narrow gap, but then nothing happens.

A frustrated cry explodes from someone trying to force their way into the room.

The rifle disappears, and an arm soon reappears with a handgun. The gun fires wildly in several directions.

Each boom causes everybody to flinch and shrink back as far as they can. Those getting crushed in the back cry out but press back further still, until their backs meet the cabinets lining the far end.

The figure disappears, taking the gun with it.

The door meekly clicks shut again.

Another silence falls.

Chapter 19:
Bonus

Monday, 2:09 p.m.
Brantford Regional High School
Brantford Township, New Jersey

Ian's down the first flight of stairs leading to the science wing before the sound of sobbing stops him on the middle landing. Glancing up, he sees only stairs. Retracing his steps up a few stairs, he spots a boy wearing a white Wild Horse Players T-Shirt. He's scrunched up in the corner of the top landing next to the emergency wheelchair. The terror in the boy's eyes angers Ian.

Pulling the handgun out from under his sweatshirt, Ian points it up at the kid.

Although shaking, the boy is too frightened to move. His eyes are clenched shut.

"Look at me," Ian orders.

The boy scrunches his shoulders, trying to pull his head in like a turtle.

"Look at me!" Ian's repeated command gets no response. Disgusted, he shoots the boy in the right shoulder.

That gets a response.

It also knocks the kid into the wheelchair.

The boy's eyes fly open, and his left hand clamps down over the wound. He stares up at Ian, silently begging for mercy.

Ian recognizes the kid's face but can't recall a name. The school is not that big. The kid's a freshman, like Sherri. His medium brown hair sticks out in many directions like he runs his hands through it frequently. The face is pockmarked from acne, and his nose is too wide.

Aware he's wasting time, Ian weighs the kid's fate.

Live or die?

He wonders if he can even afford to let the kid live. Ian has a goal to abide by.

Eighteen.

He probably came close between the first two classrooms he hit. But wounded people don't count. He needs confirmed kills.

It's better to go over the goal than not meet it.

Ian shoots the boy again.

Returning to his lacrosse bag, which got left on the middle landing, Ian pauses to reload both guns. He still had four shots left in the handgun, but he's going to need every shot going into the next fight. A mental image of coins flying out of the body and adding to an unseen counter passes through Ian's head. The idea amuses him.

He pictures bold white letters spelling out: **BONUS!**

Little Miss Perfect and her sidekick had been wearing T-Shirts like Ian's latest kill. Wild Horse Players would be worth bonus points. Their brand new white T-Shirts with a stupid mask-wearing version of the school logo make easy targets.

The decision solidifies in his head as Ian pushes through the double doors leading to the science wing.

Turning left, he jogs to room 104, drops the ammunition bag again, and tries the door handle.

To his surprise, it swings open, but a bulky Chromebook cart blocks the way.

After slamming his AR-15 against the cart, Ian decides he can't risk damaging his precious gun. Instead, he puts his left shoulder into moving the cart. It skids a few inches then stops. The gap's not wide enough to let him pass. He considers jumping over the cart but doesn't want to do so with the rifle in his hands.

Backing up, Ian charges forward and rams into the cart. His right shoulder bears the beating this time, making the fingers on his right hand go numb. The cart skids another few inches. Though not much, it's enough. Ian turns the wheels enough to slide the cart right, allowing him access to the room. Much of the cart still blocks the way, but there's a narrow path around the long lab bench and desk taking up the front of the room.

He scans the room. As expected, the classroom is empty. It's dark, but enough light leaks in through the shades to let him see. The science classrooms are much bigger than the English ones because of the lab benches.

Jogging through the slim path, Ian circumvents the five rows of desks and heads for the prep room.

He meets another door.

This handle turns too, but as soon as he starts pushing, Ian meets resistance.

Surprised, he ends up firing a short burst into the ceiling.

Muffled screams confirm that there are people beyond this flimsy door.

Slamming his body against the door, Ian feels it give way then bounce back.

Somebody must be physically blocking the door.

Smiling at the challenge, Ian retreats three steps, drawing even with the end of the last lab bench, and levels his AR-15 at the door. Due to his recent fight with the Chromebook cart, Ian's shoulder aches fiercely with each bullet that exits the gun.

But the pain's worth it to hear the panic level rise from within the tiny room. Once he gets in, it'll be easier than shooting fish in a barrel. The poor fish would have some water to swim around in. The people in that room are trapped with nowhere to go.

After emptying the entire magazine into the door, Ian moves forward and again tries to open the door. Much like the cart, he succeeds to a point. A three-inch gap appears before the door jams against something and stops.

Anger blazes inside him.

Ian throws his entire body into the door, leading with his left shoulder this time. The gap widens for a second before snapping back to three inches. He sticks the gun barrel inside and fires.

It clicks on empty.

The anger made him forget to reload.

Bellowing like a wounded animal, Ian puts down the rifle on the lab bench, draws the handgun out, and empties it into the crowded room. After the third time pulling the trigger to an empty click, Ian tucks the handgun away. Then, he recovers his rifle and pops out the empty magazine. After putting in a fresh one, he sticks the muzzle into the room and fires semi-blindly, sweeping left and right to cover as much area as possible.

The sound of breaking glass and soft sobbing fills the air.

Ian spends several seconds drawing deep breaths before reloading his guns and contemplating the door.

He can fight his way in, but if he does that, he needs to be prepared to make it his last stand. He's wasting too many bullets.

They've blocked this door.

There's a small chance the other side is less fortified, but he'll have to shoot off the lock to 106 first. Each of these tasks will take time.

He could also try talking.

"Liana," he calls gently through the opening.

"Ian?" The answer carries horror, disbelief, and fear.

"Come by the door," says Ian.

"Don't you dare," counters a commanding female voice. Ian doesn't immediately recognize it.

"What do you want, Ian?" asks Liana.

"I just want to talk," he lies.

Sounds of a struggle come from within.

"What if he's telling the truth?" wonders Liana.

"He's not." This time, Ian recognizes the female voice as HK, his chemistry teacher. "You don't fire first then ask to talk."

"Come out and I won't kill the rest of them," Ian promises.

"She can't," says HK. "You jammed the door."

"There's another door," Ian insists.

"Also blocked," says HK. "You're not getting in here."

The sound direction of HK's voice finally has meaning for Ian. Picking up the rifle he checks that it's loaded and ready. Kneeling by the door, he speaks quietly through the gap.

"Send Liana out through the other door, or I'll shoot through this one," says Ian. "I know you're sitting right behind it."

Chapter 20:
No Deal

Monday, 2:13 p.m.
Brantford Regional High School
Brantford Township, New Jersey

Through the narrow gap between the book stack and the door, Naomi sees a very pale Liana Ackerman struggle to stand, but Alycia clings to the girl with a death-grip.

Carefully, Naomi shuffles forward a few inches, drawing even with the book stack. Every muscle in her throat tries to close, but she swallows hard and forces words out. She might as well; they could be her last.

"No deal."

She scoots forward more.

A single shot barrels through the door and plows into the stored weigh boats and matches.

Naomi yelps instinctively along with half the students.

Everybody who can see her draws a collective breath and holds it.

She raises a shaky hand to her lips.

Another shot rings out.

This time, hot pain skips across the back of her neck. It feels like she got stung by a dozen ticked off wasps. Holding in a cry, Naomi grips the back of her neck. The pain intensifies, and her vision clouds. She releases the grip and tries to control the sudden urge to vomit. Shifting to her hands and knees, Naomi holds as still as possible and wills the world to stop spinning.

"Don't make me come in there!" Ian growls. The door starts to swing inward but jams again on the well-placed book. "I swear I'll kill everybody."

Nobody responds to him.

Naomi silently prays he'll go away.

Guilt creeps over her when he actually leaves. Having him outside their door is terrifying. Having him loose elsewhere in the school is disconcerting and terrifying.

Where will he go next?

A long, tense half-minute passes in relative silence.

"Is everybody okay?" Naomi whispers the question, afraid too much noise will draw Ian back.

"You're bleeding," says a dazed girl.

"Yes, but I'm still breathing, so it can't be that bad," Naomi replies. In truth, she's riding a wave of adrenaline and knows it's going to crash sooner rather than later.

"Stay put," says Alycia.

Naomi can't tell whom she's addressing, but since moving isn't high on her list of things to do anyway, she obeys.

A moment later, Alycia's by her side, gently brushing hair away from her neck.

Each strand of hair that touches the wound feels like a sharp needle.

"Is it bad?" asks Naomi. A trickle of something warm and wet sliding down her neck tells her it's probably still bleeding. Tiny dark spots dance across her vision, warning her she's probably going to pass out soon.

"Bad enough," Alycia answers tightly.

Belatedly, Naomi recalls her friend's aversion to blood.

"Okay. Fair warning. Don't want to alarm you. I'm about to pass out." Naomi eases herself to the ground. It's not terribly comfortable, but a whole lot less painful than lying down on the wound.

"This is going to hurt," Alycia says.

A second later, something lands over the wound, feeling like a hot brand. A moan slips out and sweat breaks out across Naomi's brow.

"What is—" Naomi turns sideways to look up at her friend.

"Hold still," says Alycia. She rips off a generous swatch of neon green lab tape and wraps it around the makeshift bandage. "Not long enough." She tears off a longer piece and places this over the first, completely encircling Naomi's neck.

With the wound covered, Naomi cautiously rolls onto her back and rests her head on the ground.

"How are we doing?" she asks.

"Is everybody all right?" Alycia calls, turning the question on her students.

Naomi's not too surprised when only one or two confirmations answer the question. The kids are probably in shock. Much as she would like to take a nap, Naomi knows she must move. If they let full shock take over the room, there could be dire consequences.

"Help me up," says Naomi.

"What? No. Just stay there," orders Alycia.

Naomi starts to shake her head, but the first movement sends fresh pain across her neck, bringing tears to her eyes.

"We have to keep them alert or they won't be able to respond to rescuers," says Naomi. Seeing the blood on her hands, she wipes off what she can on a paper towel since Alycia left the roll sitting next to her.

"We need to leave. We need to leave." The mantra comes from a girl huddled just out of Naomi's line of vision.

"And we need to keep them calm," Naomi adds.

They fought very hard to keep Ian out, but if panic sets in, they would end up fighting to keep these kids inside. They also needed to take stock of the situation, including the injuries.

Chapter 21:
Blue Light

Monday, 2:13 p.m.
Brantford Regional High School
Brantford Township, New Jersey

Faith Moffitt puts on her left turn signal and waits patiently for three cars to meander by. Once her way is clear, she pulls into the long, circular drive leading up to the school. Half a gym class wanders around the track while the others play kickball or wiffle ball or something pseudo-baseball. She wonders if her son is out among them. It's tough to remember his schedule with the rotating drops. She barely remembers her own schedule.

Where did the years go?

It seems like just yesterday her baby took his first steps.

Pulling into the faculty lot, Faith finds spot 18 and parks. Although she doesn't have any classes left to teach today at the high school, she wants to be ready to help her friend, Carol Reese, after school. The woman's absolutely brilliant as a theater teacher but rubbish when it comes to taking her grand visions and turning them into actual set pieces. Thankfully, the theater clubs and art classes feature a few highly talented students eager and willing to help her bring the set pieces to life.

As soon as she closes and locks her car, Faith spots her phone hanging out in its little holder on her dashboard. Force of habit made

84

her put it there even though the trip from the middle school to the high school only took four minutes. After retrieving her phone, she strolls slowly toward the side entrance.

She's still about forty feet away when she notices the blue flashing light that indicates a lockdown. She squints and her hands fly up to shield her eyes from the bright sunlight.

The light's definitely flashing.

Did I miss an email?

It's quite possible since Faith doesn't get a chance to check her email regularly throughout most workdays. The school administration is usually decent about giving the faculty and staff a warning of pending drills.

Retreating to her car, Faith tries to check her email. When that fails, she forces herself out of her car and moves closer to the school building, assuming her phone's just being annoying. Her connection bars crash to nothing. Maybe she imagined it, but Faith believes she had a bar while sitting in her car.

That's bizarre.

She ponders the situation as she strolls back to her car, eyes glued to her phone. As she draws even with her car, a single bar flickers then dies again. Frowning, Faith stares back at the school. They've had some connection issues but usually that's the difference between one and three bars. Nothing like this.

Where are the cops?

If it was a drill, the cops should already be at the scene.

The blue light still flashes its silent warning to stay out of the building, effectively trapping Faith outside on a gorgeous day. An odd feeling in her gut has her scrolling over to her son's cell number before she remembers the connection troubles. Having little else to do, she jogs across the short strip of grass leading up to the sidewalk, glances left and right, and crosses the road into the large church parking lot. She checks her phone again. The single bar returns, flickers again, and fades. Hope, curiosity, and unease make her stomach flutter even more. She questions how long the bar lasted this time.

A second. Maybe two?

Deciding she still has a legitimate excuse for not going inside, Faith chooses to indulge her curiosity a little longer. Using quick steps, she moves farther from the school. As expected, the connection improves to one bar by the time she reaches the actual church building.

A minute ticks by while Faith argues with herself. She doesn't want to call Lucas's number if it is a drill, but is it a drill? If it's not a drill, should she call him? She'd never forgive herself if calling him got him killed. The weird sensation in her stomach has graduated to full-blown anxiety. Should she call the school or the cops or just wait it out?

She tries the school first but gets nothing through eight rings.

Unfortunately, she doesn't know the number for the local police station. She should, but she doesn't.

Swallowing hard, Faith dials 911 and silently prays they don't think she's a stark raving idiot.

A woman answers on the second ring.

"911 operator. My name is Tess. What is the nature of your emergency?"

"Hi. I-I'm at the school in Brantford and there's a blue light flashing, but no cops," says Faith. "Is that normal? I called the school, but nobody's picking up. Is it a drill? Am I missing something?"

"All right, ma'am. Stay calm. Which school are you calling about?" Tess's voice settles into a cool, professional rhythm.

"Brantford Regional. The high school, not the middle school. Is it a drill? I need to know if it's a drill. My son's inside." Faith's breaths come faster and faster as the conversation continues. She glances down the hill longingly toward her car where she left her asthma medicine.

"If you're not inside, where are you, ma'am?" asks Tess.

"I'm in the parking lot of St. Mary's Church, across the street from the school. My phone wasn't working in the school lot so I came here." Faith's words spill out before she can catch her breath.

"What's your name, ma'am?" The operator's question is downright slow by comparison.

"Faith."

"All right, Faith. You're doing great. Do me a favor and stay on the line. I'm dispatching officers to your location now. Do you see anybody around you?"

"There are some kids on the field by the track," says Faith. "They're in gym class."

"Do you see a teacher with them?" asks the operator.

"Not from here, but I did on the way in," answers Faith. "Should I go to them?"

A short silence ensues.

"No. That's not necessary. Are you in a safe location?"

"I don't know!" Faith cries. "There's nobody here!"

"You're okay, Faith. Please stay where you are. Tell me exactly what you saw since you arrived at the school."

Chapter 22:
Deception

Frantic thoughts chase Ian from room 104. He hadn't wanted to shoot HK, but she had it coming for getting in his way. Not killing Liana bothers Ian, but the moment has passed. He will never make it to the other side of the school, so the head bully boy gets to live too. The best thing Ian can do now is to make one heck of a last statement before entering the endgame. To do that, he needs to break into a new room, preferably one where they've not barricaded themselves in the prep room.

Upon reaching the hallway, Ian glances left, right, and straight ahead. The nearest room is 105. The hallway's still deserted. It's strange and sad to see it so completely empty. Normally, there would be a few students or teachers wandering about, gazing into display cases or staring down at phones on the way to complete one errand or another.

He studies the locked door to the room across the hall.

What would bring people back?

Ian knows as well as anybody what protocol tells teachers to do, but he is also certain that no crappy training they received truly prepared them for him. Pride makes him smile. It's like a dream come true.

Shaking himself, Ian wipes the stupid grin off his face. There's still a lot of work to do.

Inspiration makes his breath catch. After squirreling away as much of his remaining ammunition in various pockets and around his waistband, Ian jogs to 105's door and crouches low. Forming a fist, he pounds on the door three times. Not finding the right angle to really smack the door, he stands and clutches the rifle in his left hand only.

"Help! Help! Please! I'm gonna die!" Ian follows the words up with more strikes to the door. "You have to help me!" The three-week acting course he took when he was eight comes back to him, letting him channel the heightened emotions into authentic-sounding panic.

A few more rounds of pounding and pleas get rewarded by a brief shifting in the shade covering the door.

"I'm sorry. I can't let you in!" calls a man's nervous voice through the door. "Go hide in one of the restrooms until this is over."

"He's going to kill me!" Ian says. He's mildly impressed that the teacher can resist his pleas.

Shouldering his rifle, Ian levels the weapon at the center of the glass window.

"I'm sorry—"

The man never gets to finish.

Ian imagines the guy's body arcing backwards and striking the sink on the nearest lab bench.

Unfortunately, the bullet traveled too fast, drilling a hole through the glass instead of blasting it to pieces.

Show time.

Regretting what he's about to do to his poor rifle, Ian draws it back and slams the back end hard into the glass. Urgency lends him strength to swing the weapon hard. The glass gives way so quickly his left elbow goes through before he can stop the momentum. Pain rips through his forearm, but he ignores it.

Nothing wrong with matching injuries.

After clearing out the rest of the glass with the rifle's barrel, Ian reaches through and opens the door.

He's in.

Gently, he swings the door wide and steps into 105.

Mr. Racer stares up at Ian from the floor directly in front of the first lab bench.

Drawing the handgun out of his sweatshirt pocket, Ian kneels by Mr. Racer.

"You tried," he whispers, pressing the gun to the man's forehead.

The teacher squeezes his eyes shut tight.

A heady power comes over Ian. His eyes shift left and up where the back of a picture frame faces him. Having had several classes in here, he knows the picture features Mr. Racer, a blonde woman, and three small children.

Impulsively, Ian leaps to his feet and snatches up the picture frame. Both of the man's hands clutch the bullet wound.

The moment passes.

Ian drops the frame onto the man's stomach and tucks the handgun away. Holding his rifle again with two hands makes him feel invincible. Ian has only ever had the man in a study hall, but his laid back style made it a nice class. He can afford to be generous and let fate decide whether Mr. Racer finishes the day on the list of wounded or dead.

Mental tally says Ian has likely shot upwards of fifty people, but he suspects most will live. He awards himself a tentative thirteen kills. That means he needs to score big in this last set of rooms. Given that both sets of blinds were down, Ian knows there should be two classes of students crammed into the prep room between the classrooms, just like between 104 and 106. Only this time, there won't be a stack of books blocking the door.

Victory is so close he can taste it.

The faint smell of formaldehyde taints the air, providing a fitting background scent for what's about to happen.

Running past the two sets of lab benches, Ian veers right and goes to the prep room door. The handle turns slightly but the door resists opening. A muffled yelp tells him somebody's physically holding the door closed.

Sighing, Ian steps back, brings his rifle up, and blows through half a magazine riddling the door with bullets.

Screams rise from inside the room.

Angry now, Ian rushes forward, slams down the door handle, and pushes into the room.

Chapter 23:
Distraction

"What do you suggest?" Alycia inquires, referring to Naomi's statement about keeping the kids calm.

"Feed the children," Naomi replies with a weak smile. She had to lay down again because the upright position was causing her vision to darken. "Private stashes are over there." She raises a finger to point in the general direction of her desk, realizes she's pointing aimlessly toward the ceiling, and corrects the direction. Her friend must think she's going delirious. Every move hurts her neck.

Alycia acknowledges the suggestion, carefully rises, and disappears from the space above Naomi. For a minute or two, the only sounds in the room consist of Alycia's careful footsteps, a few muffled cries, and a couple of murmured apologies. Next, comes the sounds of rustling bags and cautious crunching.

"I thought we weren't allowed to eat in a lab," says one of the boys.

I'm gonna smack him.

"Ignore him. It's not worth the time, effort, or paperwork," Alycia advises, reappearing above Naomi. "And why do you have nearly every snack food known to man?"

"Science," says Naomi, grinning at the fact that Alycia read her thought. "I wanted to see if I could get better results on the calorimetry lab."

"Pyro," Alycia comments.

"Perhaps a little," Naomi admits. "I never got around to it."

"The intent was there," says Alycia. "Do you need anything?"

"Maybe a little water." Naomi concentrates very hard on not shrugging. "They're—"

"I saw them." Alycia doesn't sound thrilled about re-crossing the sea of children to get to them.

"You mean these?" calls one of the students in a stage whisper.

"Yes, but don't—" Alycia cuts herself off and lunges over Naomi for something unseen. Something smacks hard into her hands. A pent-up breath rushes out of her. "You're lucky I have good reflexes." She glares toward where the water bottle had emanated from. "And so are you," she adds darkly.

"Sorry!" The sheepish apology comes from the same student, who must have thrown the water bottle. "But it was a toss."

Neither Alycia nor Naomi bother to answer the kid's poor excuse.

"How do you want this done?" asks Alycia.

"Just pour, I guess," says Naomi. "Very, very carefully."

Getting up again, Alycia gathers some paper towels to cover the makeshift bandage in case of a spill. Then, she carefully opens the water bottle and tries to find the best angle to hit Naomi's mouth without drenching the bandage.

After a few sips, Naomi thanks her and waves the bottle away.

"That's it?" Alycia's tone carries mild offense.

"Given we might be stuck in here for a few more hours without access to a restroom, yes," says Naomi. "But if you could put a little on a paper towel, I'd be grateful."

"Good point," Alycia admits, "and sure." She pours some water on the wad of paper towel Naomi had used to clean her hands before and gives it to her. Next, she cautiously sips from the water bottle before replacing the cap and resting it on the floor near Naomi. "It'll be here if you need more."

"Can we leave now?" The unseen female speaker sounds a hair shy of a mental breakdown.

"Not yet," Alycia answers.

"Is she going to die?" asks the same speaker.

"Not yet," Naomi answers, not bothering to raise her head.

Instead, she lifts one of her arms off her stomach where it had been resting.

"We need to leave. Please! I need—"

"Shut up!" calls one of the boys.

"Hey, try to be a little sensitive!" scolds another girl.

"I am not spending the next few hours with her whining the whole time," argues the same boy.

Alycia and Naomi exchange a look.

"Better help me up," says Naomi. "United front and all that jazz."

The process of rising requires way more effort than it ought to, but oddly, the task becomes a community building exercise that momentarily silences debate. Several students help shift over a stack of textbooks, but it proves too unstable to provide adequate support. Once the space is cleared again, one of the students sits down behind Naomi. She keeps her head tilted forward to keep from pressing on the wound. Nevertheless, she carefully leans back against the unknown student.

"Mom!" chirps the student, clarifying matters.

"Hi, Joey. Thanks for the support." Naomi never could guess why this random child, clearly not her son, insists on calling her such.

"No problem," says Joey.

It's a little odd to be facing away from somebody she's talking to, but Naomi gets over the weird factor in a hurry by concentrating on the crowd of worried faces in front of her.

"First thing's first, is anybody else injured?" Naomi asks.

A few students report bruises from being shoved and stepped on by their peers, and three bear cuts from flying glass. Some of the non-injured students help bandage the wounds with paper towels and lab tape. Once the first aid needs are addressed, Naomi begins her calming speech. Those were never her strong suit, but these kids are about as close to cracking as she feels.

"We'll be all right. The worst part is over." Part of Naomi feels guilty because the scattered gunshots that have become the norm say the problem has merely moved elsewhere.

The kids have even stopped flinching at single gunshots.

"Best thing we can do now is stay put," Alycia adds. "The police will be here as soon as they can."

The fear in the students' eyes haunts Naomi.

Any suggestions, God? she wonders silently.

The answer is immediate and emphatic: music.

"Now I want you to listen to me very carefully, because it's not something you're going to hear often. Take out your phones and load up something classical and soothing. If you don't have a saved list, find somebody who does. Nothing hard. Nothing loud. Preferably something without words. Just music."

After a brief discussion, she discovers that only a handful of students have music fitting those requirements. Naomi weighs the consequences of making noise against letting everybody's nerves continue to fray. Deciding to take the risk, she retrieves her phone from the pocket she'd stuffed it in earlier and gingerly pokes the screen until the machine finds her non-lyric favorites list.

Soon, gentle violin music fills the quiet room.

Several students scoot closer to hear because Naomi's not turning the volume up much past three bars.

Alycia distributes water, tissues, and the remaining snacks, along with fair warning that they could still be stuck for a few hours. Inevitably, a few voice a need to use the restroom.

"Try to sleep." The advice comes from Alycia, but Naomi has nothing better to suggest.

She really doesn't want to think about what happens if rescue takes another few hours.

Chapter 24:
First Responder

Monday, 2:17 p.m.
Broadway Avenue
Brantford Township, New Jersey

Officer Sean Burgess smashes the gas pedal to the floor and then leans hard on the brakes as he approaches an intersection where the light currently shines red in his direction. He engages the sirens. Slowing only briefly to make sure he doesn't get crushed, Sean sails through the intersection and dodges around a few vehicles just noticing his hurry. He cuts the sirens but keeps the light bar swirling.

"Out of the way. Out of the way." Normally, Sean enjoys the thrill of blasting beyond speed limits and running red lights, but today, he wishes he could teleport to the destination. The sleepy, winding streets prevent him from truly testing the cruiser's top speeds.

He doesn't personally have a child at the high school but several of his colleagues do. His wife, Jennifer, works at one of the local elementary schools, and he likes to think a similar situation would prompt an urgent response from any of his fellow officers. The slim details he received thus far are sketchy at best, yet still terrifying. The high school went into a lockdown without tripping the alarms at the station. Even a complete power outage shouldn't be able to accomplish such a feat.

Pulling into the paved lane leading up to the high school, Officer

Burgess keeps alert for any signs of trouble. Several kids gather along the track fence and gawk at his vehicle and the flashing lights. Their teacher half-heartedly tries to get their attention, but it's a lost cause. Sean hopes the spectators have enough sense to stay put because he doesn't have the time to warn them off.

Pulling up to the front door, Sean parks and reaches for his radio mike to report his position.

Faint static comes through the line, chilling him to his core. Whipping out his cell phone, he tries to call 911, but that doesn't work either. Although warned the original 911 caller had connection troubles, Sean never dreamed the effects would extend to his radio.

Exiting his vehicle, Sean tries the phone again.

Nothing.

Rapid popping noises reach his ears. He's torn between the need to rush headlong into the school and the instinct to report his position. Stepping into the unknown with no backup is foolish, but if those pops turn out to be gunshots, his primary job must be saving lives.

Three more pops sound before Sean reaches a decision and unsticks his feet from the pavement. Leaving the car door open, he draws his service weapon and dashes to the front door.

It's locked.

Eight more noises imitating far-off firecrackers reach him. Digging around in his left pocket, Sean retrieves the giant ring of keys and stares at them. He can't remember which color represents the high school key. There has never been a need for it before now. Usually, when he drops by to stroll through the hallways, there's a lady at the front desk ready to buzz him in.

It's not orange. That one is Jennifer's favorite color, so it goes to Casement Elementary where their seven-year-old son attends school.

Green's another of the elementary schools.

The sound of gunshots pierces his concentration.

Wincing at the consequences of further delay, Sean sends up a silent prayer for inspiration.

Gray.

The key identifier he's looking for is gray. Slipping the correct key into the slot, Sean unlocks the door and enters the school. He stuffs his keys back into his pocket and grips his gun two-handed. Instinctively, he bends his knees like someone sneaking around and moves toward the left side of the wide hallway.

His gaze takes in everything. The reception desk has been

abandoned. The doors to the two theaters remain closed. The first hallway he comes to is clear of people.

A gunshot draws his attention to the next hallway on the left.

Dropping to a full crouch, Sean peeks around the corner.

At first, nothing seems amiss.

A string of loud gunshots quickly changes his mind.

He stares down at the service weapon. The Glock 22 is most definitely outmatched here, but that doesn't change his objective.

The gunshots change tone from quick chatter to slower single shots. The methodical nature of these new shots opens a pit of dread within Sean.

A million movies lines sail through him, but Officer Burgess pushes them aside.

His hands tremble.

Somewhere down that hallway bad things are happening. He never asked to be in a situation like this, but it's here and so is he.

Self-preservation would tell him to get down that hallway and wait for the perpetrator to emerge from the room before ambushing him. But that option does not exist for Sean. Clearing his mind, he pushes to his feet and sprints toward the gunfire. He doesn't bother masking the sound of his footfalls.

Maybe a movie line will help him.

"Police! We have you surrounded!" Sean bellows as loud as he can. "Throw down your weapons and come out with your hands up."

He's leaning on the lockers just outside the room with the gunfire.

Six shots zip out the door and slam into lockers across from Scan.

He waits and weighs his options. Bursting in would likely be suicide. By the time his eyes adjust to the dim lights within, the gunman will have ample opportunities to pick him off.

A mental image of Jacob comes to mind. Sean pictures his son's face pinched in concentration as he catches a baseball. The scene shifts to their last family trip to the beach. Jacob and Jordana had insisted on getting their feet wet even though the water had been freezing.

Sean comforts himself with the knowledge that his kids are far from this madness, but other people aren't so lucky today.

The hairs on the back of his neck tingle.

Dropping flat onto his stomach, Sean rolls right so that he's on his back.

Three bullets pass through the space he'd just abandoned.

He fires blindly. The two shots go wide but they send the figure scrambling back inside the room.

"All units converge on my position!" Sean shouts, desperately wishing for other units. He doubts the shooter is listening, but he needs every edge he can get right now.

A figure bursts out of the first room and sprints away before Sean recovers his feet.

He's grateful to be alive, but now, he has another awful choice to make. He can—and should—pursue the shooter, but part of him needs to assess the damage done thus far. People could be dying this very instant, alone and afraid. No kid deserves that fate.

Heart tearing in two, Sean finishes standing and cautiously runs to where the hallway branches off to the right.

He arrives in time to see the boys' restroom door closing.

Any doubts about the person being the shooter vanish when a single gunshot rings out from inside the lavatory.

Chapter 25:
Calm

Parking Lot of St. Mary's Church
Brantford Township, New Jersey

Faith Moffitt alternates straining her eyes to watch the front doors of the high school and pacing back and forth across a small patch of grass. She had lost the connection with Tess, the 911 operator, and wandered too close to the dead zone to allow a new connection to be established. From this distance, she can't see much. The cop car still sits out front with its door ajar.

Nervous energy interferes with rational thought. She wants to call somebody, but who would she call? What could she say to them if she did call somebody?

Hi, something bad might be going on at the high school. No, I don't know anything more than that.

Her hands are trembling too badly to let her access the correct menus on her phone even if her husband, Scott, was available this afternoon. She couldn't recall his exact reason until she thought about it very hard for almost a minute.

Court. Scott would be litigating a big case today. He always silences his phone on court days.

Another cop car arrives. This one offloads two officers. The distance prevents Faith from hearing actual words, but she gathers from their gestures that they're also having trouble with their radios.

Jammer!

Faith tries desperately to recall if she mentioned the possibility to Tess. Given that she can barely recall her own name, she doubts it, but they need to know. Scott had been babbling about some article that mentioned phone jammers just the other day. Unfortunately, only his general sense of amusement remains of the conversation.

Should she speak to the cops? They look amped up enough to turn on her, but she can't let them go in blind.

Paint the whole picture.

Her own advice breaks through the panic long enough to level her emotions. The advice has a way different context here, but the idea fits.

One of the cops disappears into the building before Faith can move a muscle anyway. The other hops in the driver's seat and drives across the school's manicured front lawn.

Path clear now, Faith wheels around and sprints toward the parking lot and the church building. Once she's dead center of the large, empty parking lot, Faith dials 911 again.

There's a slight delay after the call connects, but shortly thereafter, Tess's voice comes through loud and clear.

"Faith? Are you all right? We lost the connection before. Has anything changed?"

"Tell me the truth, is this for real?"

"Officers are on scene investigating as we speak," replies Tess.

Faith starts hyperventilating.

"Faith, talk to me," says Tess. "Repeat after me: 'I am all right.' Can you do that? Concentrate on the words."

"I'm all right. I'm all right." The short chant calms Faith a little, kickstarting her brain and reminding her of the purpose of this second call. "But there's a jammer in the school!"

"We know," says Tess. "Responding officers are being warned of the possibility. Just stay calm and let the officers do their jobs."

"Two of them went in!" Faith shouts. "I don't think any of their radios worked! What do I do? My son's in there!"

"You're doing exactly what you need to do." Tess's tone walks a fine line between being firm and soothing. "More units will be there shortly. Keep talking to me and stay on the line. Officer Kiernan will be with you shortly. Tell me about your son. What's his name? Where is he located in the building? I'll relay the information to the police."

"His name is Lucas. I don't know where he is. I don't know his

100

schedule! I need to make some calls. Others will want to know what's happening."

"No." Tess's voice edges higher with urgency. "Faith, listen to me. Alerting others could hamper the rescue efforts and endanger more people. If necessary, there will be a rescue effort, but the officers need to sweep the school to make sure it's safe for others to enter. We don't even know if that's necessary, but we have to guess, given the circumstances."

"I have to do something," Faith says. "I need to see my son!"

"You have done something," Tess assures Faith, "and you will see your son. But right now, nobody knows what's going on inside that school. Until we figure that out, we have no idea how much help we're going to need. We're going to hope for the best and plan for the worst. The roads need to stay clear, and that won't happen if we have a hundred worried parents trying to get into the school."

"You're going to have that problem anyway soon," Faith argues. "School ends in half an hour."

"Help Officer Kiernan direct parents to your location," says Tess. "Keep them calm and out of the way so she can direct the emergency crews that will be arriving shortly. Call me back if you need to."

Faith stares at her phone, trying to process the call.

"You must be Faith. I'm Officer Kiernan."

The new female voice brings Faith's head up from her phone in a hurry. She flinches as the police officer extends a hand to shake. Ignoring the hand, Faith wanders back to the edge of the parking lot where she can see the school.

"I'm told we have you to thank for the notification," says Officer Kiernan, keeping pace with Faith. "Name's Bonnie. You can use that if you prefer."

Faith looks at the young officer incredulously. Her friendly, almost cheerful manner annoys Faith. Her art teacher side kicks in long enough to absorb relevant details. The officer's blond hair is neatly pinned atop her head and tucked under a wide, dark blue cap. She's got half a head's height on Faith's five-foot, three inches.

"How can you be this calm?"

"Part of the job, ma'am," replies Kiernan. A look of concern replaces the cool professional armor for a moment. She lowers her voice. "I'm worried too. My partner's in there and out of reach. And I've got a cousin in there too. She's only seventeen."

"Don't you want to be in there?" Faith demands.

"Of course," Officer Kiernan answers. "My gut wants to charge forward, but my orders are to establish a perimeter and keep civilians out of harm's way. I need to go set up some cones and flares, but when people start showing up, I'm going to send them up here. Will you help them?"

"How can I help?" Faith asks, feeling helpless.

Officer Kiernan shrugs.

"I'm honestly not sure. Distract them, I guess," she says. "Try to organize them as best you can so we can facilitate reunions as quickly as possible when that time comes. More officers will arrive soon, but we're going to need a lot of help today."

The thought of such an enormous task nearly overwhelms Faith.

"Looks like you have your first customers," Officer Kiernan says gently.

Following the officer's nod, Faith sees a couple dozen students being herded across the street by their gym teacher. It takes Faith's stressed brain several seconds to generate a name for the face. Kelly VanDaley shoos the students further up the lawn before approaching Faith and Officer Kiernan.

"Can I send some of the students home?" Kelly asks the police officer. "Only like two of them have their car keys, but I'd like to get them out of here."

Officer Kiernan looks troubled, but she recovers quickly.

"Better keep them together as best you can," says Officer Kiernan. "Their folks are going to want to know where to find them. Is the main building unlocked?"

"I don't know," Faith answers.

Kelly too admits to not knowing the answer, but she dispatches one of the students to find out.

"Can I borrow your phone?" inquires Kelly, pointing to the item clutched in Faith's sweaty palm.

Faith looks to the officer and waits for permission.

"Who do you need to call?" asks the officer.

"My husband. I need to let him know I'm safe," says Kelly.

"He probably doesn't even know anything's wrong yet," Officer Kiernan points out, shaking her head against the idea of making unnecessary phone calls. "There's a problem with communication around the school."

"He'll know." Kelly's tone leaves no room for doubt. "He's a radio hobbyist. And he monitors police frequencies."

"It's very important that we avoid a panic—"

A girl's angry words cut off the officer's protest.

"I don't know! Just come get me! We're locked out of the school."

Officer Kiernan sighs.

"So much for avoiding panic." Turning to Faith and Kelly, she adds, "Let them call their parents if you wish, but try to limit it to one or two phones in use at any given time. It won't help anybody if the cell tower gets overloaded now."

The possibility had never even occurred to Faith, but once voiced, it rips through her like a chill wind.

Chapter 26:
Regrouping

"Stop screaming," Ian orders calmly.

The kid subsides for a short while before rambling.

"Please don't kill me. I don't want to die." He's on the floor near the sinks clutching at his right foot where Ian shot him.

Ian knows the face, but he can't put a name to it. He's a freshman, but he doesn't play sports, have a significant part in any clubs, or had his face blasted up on the televisions as student of the month. Still, the school's small enough that their paths cross in the hallways every few days.

"Shhhh. Stop talking so I can think." Ian attempts to keep his voice steady and calm. He hadn't meant to come in here, but the unexpected encounter with the cop threw off his carefully laid plan. He'd abandoned the lacrosse bag in the hallway, but that doesn't matter since he already took all the ammunition out of it. Blind luck brought him to a place where he'd stored more ammunition, but the boys' room isn't exactly an ideal place to host a last stand.

The boy confines his noises to whimpers, which are still annoying but less so than the pleas or the screams.

Ian eyes the door nervously. There's no way to bar the door effectively. If he had a textbook, he might be able to jam the door like

HK had done in the prep room, but what then? The restroom's a dead end. The only way out is through the door he just entered, and the cop's bound to be there soon, if he's not already there.

He could run. If he fires through the door, the cop will cower, seek cover, or be hit. Any of those options should clear the way for a brief time. There's a set of doors left of the restroom that lead to the courtyard next to the media center. If Ian can get out through there, he should be able to access the front parking lot.

Somebody will see me.

Ian almost smiles at the ridiculous thought. The chemistry students he failed to kill already identified him. It's only a matter of time before they tell the police. If he uses the ammo from the backpack, he can probably take over one more classroom. That would give him a lot more bargaining power than a single hostage, but to what end?

What do I want?

He surprises himself by circling back to that question.

"Let me go," says the kid.

Do I have enough kills?

Ian eyes the kid seriously and levels his gun at him.

"Sorry, kid. Going for a record here."

He fires.

The single gunshot echoes in the confined space.

Practically hearing a clock tick in his head, Ian scrambles into the back stall and reloads both guns. Then, he straps the backpack on and faces the door. Collecting his scattered courage, Ian fires a short burst through the door at mid height then barrels through and fires a few times to the right before ultimately turning left. A gunshot strikes the door above his head.

"Freeze!"

The man's order only spurs Ian on faster.

He ducks instinctively, turns, and fires a few more times toward the voice. At the same time, he jogs backwards as quickly as possible. Skidding to a halt by the media center, Ian pauses only long enough to send a line of bullets through the glass doors. They shatter. Lacking the time to admire his work, Ian shoulders through some of the remaining glass and steps into the quiet space beyond.

He looks left then right and fantasizes about shooting Ms. Sandie, the cranky librarian, but she's nowhere in sight. Sunlight streaming in from the double doors leading to the courtyard nearly blinds him. Going right would lead him to the computers. The only place that might have a crowd of people, would be the computer lab, but only if there's a class there currently.

It's a gamble.

No, it's not.

Ian suddenly remembers that two-thirds of the Trio have social studies in the Glass Lab this period. He grins. Hearing footsteps in the hall, Ian whirls and faces the glass doors he just broke through. They offer no defense. He's not ready to give up just yet.

Dashing right, Ian runs to the rickety door separating the Glass Lab from the rest of the media center. Muffled cries reward him when he breaks through. The entire room is lined with students crouched under desks.

Enough sneaking around.

Flipping on the lights, Ian shouts orders. He's vastly outnumbered in a cramped space. He's got to gain control quickly.

"Everybody stand up and move to the back wall!"

He fires once through the ceiling. The crowd flinches then moves, directed by frantic motions from Ian. Two holdouts too scared to climb out from under the desks cling to each other, eyes clenched shut.

Disobedience equals consequence.

Drawing the handgun, Ian quickly shoots the two not quick enough to comply. The teacher, Mr. Wright, tries to intervene, but backs down when Ian turns the gun on him.

"Back off," Ian says.

"Colt?" The question comes from one of the burly students lining the back wall. "Didn't think you'd have—"

"Shut it, Ryman," snaps Mr. Wright, keeping both his hands raised.

"Ryman, welcome," says Ian. "Let's hold a trial. Curt Ryman, guilty." Ian punctuates the statement with a bullet. The class comes alive with scattered screams. "Max Kessler, guilty." A second shot rings out but it finds Mr. Wright instead of its intended target.

Every eye follow the man's body to the floor.

"That was pointless," Ian mutters, adjusting his aim.

Max holds up both hands to ward off the inevitable.

The bullet drops him to the floor.

One of the girls faints. Another struggles to catch her and ease her down to the ground gently.

It's a small class. Only six students remain unharmed, including the one who fainted.

Ian needs to slow down or he'll run out of hostages before things can get interesting. A whimper comes from beneath the first desk where Ian took out the slowpokes. He considers ending the kid's misery, but bullets are now a precious and very limited commodity. Time should kill the kid eventually, especially if there's nothing to stop the bleeding.

Scanning the remaining students, Ian decides they're too spread out. He can't adequately control even six people if half of them remain out of his sight. After a minute of careful arranging, Ian has the remaining students crammed into the back right corner, away from either entrance. Choosing a room with two entrances was kind of dumb, but there's no going back now.

Further thought gives Ian a better idea. It takes some coordination, but the remaining two girls and four boys are highly motivated helpers. Soon, they build a makeshift fort from computer desks and chairs. They move monitors to the floor and collapse tables where they can to leave clear lines of sight to both doors.

The bodies of the wounded and dying are moved outside the protective circle. Only the six intact hostages and Ian are permitted inside the cozy fort. Since that's a little too close for comfort, he instructs the girls on using computer cords to tie the hands and feet of the boys. They protest, but the handgun provides enough clout to win the argument. Finally, Ian ties up the two girls.

"Now we wait," says Ian.

"For what?" asks Anabelle Lins.

"Whatever comes," Ian answers, shrugging out of the backpack. The newfound sense of control comforts him. He calmly checks his ammunition situation. He has about six or seven shots in the current handgun, a fully loaded backup in the backpack, and about five shots in the AR-15. The backpack should have held a few more magazines for the rifle, but instead, the space holds three water bottles and a box of granola bars.

It will be enough. It must be.

Chapter 27:
Reinforcements

Monday, 2:32 p.m.
Brantford Regional High School
Brantford Township, New Jersey

Officer Sean Burgess can't believe his rotten luck. The kid wasn't even aiming and still managed to hit his left leg. If he'd been shot in the chest, the bulletproof vest would have done its job. As is, he's stuck in the cross section of two hallways. He doesn't think a major artery has been hit, but the wound is deep enough to leak blood onto the white floor tiles and hurt like a branding iron shoved right through his thigh.

"Drop your weapon and put your hands up!" somebody shouts from far away. The male voice sounds agitated.

Do I look like I have my weapon? Where is my weapon?

Sean barely has the sense to turn his head. Luckily, he lacks the strength to raise his handgun, which is indeed in his hand. He blinks at the two officers approaching.

I'm on your side, idiots.

"I'm …."

Sean doesn't get far with the statement before his lightheaded state makes speaking too much of a chore to be worthwhile.

"Sarge, I think it's Sean," says another male voice. This one's younger and lighter than the previous voice.

"What's he doing there?" asks the gruffer voice.

What's it look like?

If the words came out aloud, Sean's certain they would be slurred.

"Bleeding," answers the younger officer, "a lot."

"Well, get something to stop the bleeding, Vickers," snaps Sergeant Gaits. "Where did Locke get to?"

"Last I saw, he was headed straight where we turned left," answers Vickers.

"Get me that First Aid Kit then go find Officer Locke," says Sergeant Gaits. "Find that jammer and put a bullet through it."

"Are you sure?" Vickers asks, sounding awed. His dark skin makes the whites of his eyes stand out more to Sean's pain-muddled brain.

"It means, turn it off." Sarge's tone tells Sean he's rapidly losing patience with the new kid. "First Aid Kit, now."

"Right. On it," says Vickers.

Sean's conscious enough to see Corey Vickers nodding eagerly before bounding away. He's back in less than a minute.

Must warn them.

The best Sean can manage is a moan.

"Are you sure you want me to follow Locke?" wonders Vickers.

"I'm sure I want you to get me control of the airwaves, stat," says Sergeant Gaits.

"But what if he comes back?" argues Vickers. "You'll have a heck of a problem if that happens."

"If you don't get gone now, *I'm* going to be your biggest problem." Gaits's irritation with Vickers causes his movements to be a tad rougher and swifter than they might have been otherwise.

I should rest.

Something gently slaps Sean's face.

"Hey, Burgess. Look alive! Eh, probably not the best phrase right now, but I'm serious. You need to stay awake."

Suddenly, a strong wave of peppermint smacks Sean in the face. His eyes start to tear, and he's instantly more alert.

"Sorry, fresh out of smelling salts." Sergeant Gaits sounds embarrassed. "Had to improvise. You pass out and I'll blast you again."

Even as he keeps up a steady flow of chatter, the sergeant digs through the First Aid Kit and finds the gauze wrap and a poncho. After reducing the poncho to strips, he wraps several around the open wound to hold in a wad of gauze.

"Ah ha! Look what I found." Triumph rings clear through the

sergeant's statement. He holds up a beige thing that looks like a discarded snakeskin. "Might just save your sorry behind with this beauty."

Before Sean can think too hard about what the man found, the pain explodes to a new level then settles down.

"That should slow the bleeding," explains Gaits.

Sean guessed as much, but he appreciates the man's efforts to reassure him.

"Normally, I'd stay with you, but there's a nutjob running around the place busting holes in walls and people. Can't have that on my watch."

"Down hall. Left." The words sap much of Sean's remaining strength, but he locks eyes with Gaits to let him know he's serious. "Came out. Bathroom."

"What? You got to take a leak or something?" asks Gaits.

Sean glares at the man.

"Sorry. Message received. Perp's down this hall on the left. I'll get right on that as soon as I tuck you into a safe place." Gaits stops speaking long enough to drag Sean to an open door. Even though the distance is less than ten feet, Gaits is gasping by the time they get there. "What are they feeding you guys these days? Lead weights? Nah, don't answer that. Son of a—"

The sound of a boot thudding into something large causes Sean to twist his head up and to the left.

"Sorry, Burgess. Some inconsiderate boob parked a metal monster in the way. This is as far in as you go." With one huge effort, Gaits hauls Sean up far enough to lean back against the cold metal surface of a computer cart.

"Just. Get. Him."

"10-4, buddy. Hang in there," says Gaits. "I'm going to leave the breath spray with you. If you feel yourself slipping do a short squirt near your nose. Near, not in. Remember that or you'll be in a whole new world of pain."

They clasp hands briefly, then Gaits draws his service weapon and moves cautiously back toward the cross section leading to the hallway holding the boys' room and the media center.

Several gunshots ring out followed closely by screams.

Sean tries to get up, but Gaits waves for him to stand down.

Chapter 28:
Letters

A sense of dread turns every minute into an eternity. Music calms most of the students, but several are still too keyed up to settle down. After a short conference, Alycia suggests the students write letters to their loved ones. Finding it sound advice, Naomi pulls out her phone and writes to her husband.

Dear Jack,

I can't believe it's only been four years since you came into my life. I'm hoping we can read this together later. There won't be laughter in the telling, but if I can just cry with you, I'll be content. There's so much to say, to share, to do.

I can't imagine what news of this day will do to you. I'm all right for now, but it's not over yet. Since facts are going to get muddied, I'll tell you what I know.

One of my students, Ian Colt, somehow got a few guns and, well, familiar, old American tale at this point. He came in today and unleashed his inner demons on dozens of innocents. I don't know if people died, but there has been a LOT of gunfire.

Pray for us.

No matter what happens. We're going to need it.

Hearts are shattered. Lives are altered forever.

Nobody knows when, or if, we'll get out of this.

I am ready for whatever future plays out, but so many are not.

It's not fair. It never is.

If I make it, I love you.

If I don't, I love you more. Remember that as you mourn, but also, move on in due time.

Thank you for every laugh, new adventure, and quiet moment.

The network is down, so this won't send right away. But don't worry, I will send it as soon as possible.

As of this second, I'm alive. That counts for a lot, right? :-)

Cheers.

N.

Silence reigns as each student stares into space, taps out their letters, listens to music, or simply cries. Alycia embraces a visibly shaken girl. Naomi can tell from her friend's expression that she's barely holding it together enough to support the students.

"Is it over?" pleads a girl. She sits to Naomi's left, tucked under the desk with both arms wrapped around her knees. She's rocking back and forth.

"What's your name?" asks Naomi.

"Hope." The girl's soft voice sounds loud in the still air.

"That's a perfect name," says Naomi.

The girl's only response is to blink twice. The other students stop shuffling about and watch the exchange.

"It's what we need," Naomi clarifies for the listeners.

"Are we going to die?" asks Hope.

"No." Alycia's answer sounds especially loud, as if declaring it solidly enough will turn wish into fact.

"How do you know?" Hope's question gets echoed by several murmurs.

"We don't," Naomi admits. "But we've made it this far. There's no reason to believe otherwise. Hang on to hope."

Taking her literally, the two kids nearest to Hope grab hold of her hands. At first, surprise registers on the girl's face, but she quickly squeezes back. Several others huddle in, clasping hands and moving closer like little chicks gathering for warmth.

"Be brave," says Alycia. "Remember, I love you. You drive me nuts, but I love you. We'll make it."

Naomi scans the faces she can see to gauge the impact of her colleague's words. Judging by the blank expressions, several probably didn't hear a blessed word, but many nod. They still look scared witless, but there's the faintest spark of light behind their eyes.

I hate waiting, but it does beat bullets.

Chapter 29:
Feedback

"Anything?" inquires Officer Corey Vickers.

"Still nothing." Nolan Locke's reply is curt. He fiddles with the dials on his radio. Sweat pours down his face even though the most strenuous physical thing they've done for the past eight minutes is shuffle through hallways and climb a few flights of stairs.

Corey can sympathize. The tension has each of his nerves twitching. He's surprised he can hear anything over the pounding of his heart between his ears.

"What'd the crazy lady say her husband said?" he asks.

"Something about feedback," replies Locke. He continues twisting the dials on his radio.

Suddenly, the thing emits a high-pitched screech followed by a wave of crackling static.

Yes! Static never sounded so good.

"We're getting close," says Corey.

Nolan only glares for a second before slipping the radio back into the waist holder and drawing his gun.

The sign above their heads reads: Lower Gym.

Corey moves into position next to the door and waits for Nolan to nod readiness. Carefully mouthing a countdown, Corey puts up one

114

finger, two fingers, three fingers, and then closes his fist before grabbing a hold of the door handle and swinging the thing aside.

Nolan slips through the opening, and Corey follows close on his heels.

They quickly scan the gym for threats.

Finding none out in the open, they look to each other. Nolan nods left where a sturdy, metal door leads to the boys' locker room. The entry ritual repeats, and they step through into the messy locker room unopposed. A search reveals that they're alone.

"It must be in one of the lockers," says Corey, putting his weapon away.

"Or the bags," adds Nolan. He too holsters his gun.

"Are we allowed to search those?" Corey wonders. He wracks his brain for the seminar on the legalities of searches.

Nolan just quirks an eyebrow at him.

"I'm serious, man. I don't want to lose my job over a technicality," says Corey defensively.

"Pretty sure we're covered," Nolan replies, his tone back to curt. "Search the lockers. I'll do the bags."

Corey almost asks how he should go about the task, but then, he remembers back to his days as an assistant coach.

"Be right back," he calls to his temporary partner. "Gonna go get the key."

Ducking into the tiny office next to the locker room, Corey riffles through the desk. The search yields typical office debris: spare staples, push pins, white out tape, pens, chewed up pencils, sticky notes, a small notebook, a few whistles, and binders with various labels. Releasing a frustrated sigh, Corey turns his attention to each of the other walls.

The desk occupies the wall to the right as one enters the small office. The wall straight ahead holds a large corkboard covered in papers. The left wall holds three small lockers and a coat rack, and the last wall features two chairs with dark blue cushions.

Two steps carry Corey to the lockers, but searching them turns up only a sweatshirt, a roll of sports tape, and a pack of chewing gum. Slamming the last locker door causes some of the papers to ruffle, revealing a row of small hooks. The first three are empty. Ripping off the bottom row of papers reveals more hooks. Most hold nothing, but the last four on the right hold tiny keys pinned together in pairs.

Snatching the keys, Corey books it back to the locker room and heads to the nearest locker. He trips on an empty sports bag.

Locke's been busy.

Across the room, Nolan is still ripping open bags and dumping the contents on the ground.

Reaching his destination, Corey fumbles with the lock and tries every key on it. The third he tries fits perfectly. Pulling the lock open, Corey yanks open the metal door and eagerly peers inside. A wave of foul air slams into Corey, making him choke and cough. A pile of dirty socks lies at eye level. Breathing through his mouth, he moves on.

When Nolan finishes with the sports bags, he joins Corey at the lockers.

"Too bad there's not another master key," he mutters, diving into the first locker to add its contents to the floor.

"There is," says Corey, just coming to the realization.

Nolan's eyes blaze as he sticks out his hand for the second key.

A few seconds pass while Corey struggles to separate the pair. Lacking the patience, he eventually yanks hard, causing the flimsy piece of metal holding the keys together to snap. He tosses the key to his partner and returns to his search.

Dashing to the other side, Nolan begins breaking into lockers.

Corey's head hurts from the combination of rising stench and high anxiety, but he forces himself to focus.

Insert key, twist, open.

He thinks through the steps each time to keep his mind from wandering. In fact, he's so focused that he barely notices that suddenly one of the lockers before him holds nothing but a large metal box covered in lights and dials and a discarded lacrosse bag.

"Got it!" he cries.

Nolan rushes over.

"What are you waiting for? Turn it off!" Nolan orders.

Corey's not exactly sure how to do that because the buttons have no labels. Finding some switches on the side, he flicks a few at random. Finally, he finds one that turns off the lights.

"Did it work?" he wonders.

"Let's find out," says Nolan, picking up his radio. "Sarge? Can you hear me?"

"Locke! Well done. Is Vickers with you?" asks Sergeant Gaits.

"Affirmative," replies Locke.

"Great. Get your butts down to the media center. There's another crisis brewing."

Muffled voices come through the radio, then Sergeant Gaits comes back on the line.

"Forget what I just said, continue your patrols, check every room for possible signs of trouble. I've just received new info. There could be a bomb or two out there."

Corey's eyes widen in alarm.

"Um, shouldn't we wait for a bomb squad, Sarge?" asks Locke.

"Don't have the luxury of time here," answers Gaits. "Take every precaution and then some. If you find a possible location, report it and get clear."

Chapter 30:
Desperate Connections

Monday, 2:45 p.m.
Brantford Regional High School
Brantford Township, New Jersey

"I'm through!" The triumphant declaration comes from Miguel Torres.

Megan Marquette and the rest of her classmates waste no time placing calls to their loved ones.

"Try to keep it down, people," calls Miss DeHart. "We're still under a lockdown."

Pick up. Pick up! The thought fires through Megan's head a minimum of ten times in five seconds. She strangles her phone during the painful wait for her mother to answer the call.

"Yes, dear, I'm on my way. What's the matter? You couldn't wait five minutes to see me?"

The light, teasing tone nearly brings Megan to tears.

"Mom!" A sob blossoms in her throat, making it impossible to form words.

The buzz of conversation rises around her. Frustrated, Megan clamps a hand over her left ear to block out some of the noise.

"Is everything all right?" Her mother's tone dips to a serious level. "Talk to me, Megan. There's—oh my goodness."

The screech of brakes comes faintly through the cell phone connection.

"Mom? What's wrong?" asks Megan.

Two nearby students shush her while a third glares.

"Nothing. I've never seen traffic like this out here … this must be why you're calling me." The remaining traces of levity vanish. "Full story. Right now."

Megan closes her eyes and concentrates on her mother.

"We're in a lockdown," she whispers. "We heard gunshots. So many gunshots."

Even though it's not a FaceTime connection, Megan can imagine the color draining from her mother's already pale features.

"Are you all right? Have you talked to your sister?" The questions come out so quickly they practically become one word.

"I'm okay. But we're still in a lockdown. I don't know about Valerie, but I'm scared." Megan bites her bottom lip as she contemplates sharing her fears. The twisting and turning of her stomach makes her nauseous. "Mom …."

"Yeah, baby? I'm here. I'm listening."

"The shots were close and across the hall. That's where Val is."

The sharp intake of breath from her mother stabs Megan in the heart. She holds her breath, not sure what reaction to expect from her mother.

Unable to hold back the tears, Megan lets them flow.

"I think that's where it started."

"Megan." Her mother's call is soft and filled with a note she's long come to dread.

"You're not coming," Megan says, her voice deadpan.

"When you get out, try to find your sister, but if you can't find her quickly, get to your aunt's place. I'll meet you there when I can, but if it's as bad as you think it is, I need to get back to work. They're going to need me there."

Anger replaces the fear for one blazing-hot second.

"And I need you here! Don't I count for anything?" Regretting the words immediately, Megan wrestles with her emotions, burying the jealousy and frustration as usual. She's lost track of the number of times her mother's job has taken priority over her or Val. Usually, she watches the local news channels for the tragedy that causes her mother to pull late hours at the hospital, but this time, she has first-hand knowledge of the cause. "Forget it." She tries to soften the words, but they still fly through the connection like cannon balls. Her finger hovers over the red icon that would end the call, but she can't bring herself to do it.

"I love you, Megan. Remember that. I'll have my phone with me every second. Call me every hour if you can, and call immediately if you hear from your sister. Did you try calling her?"

"No, but I will." A shot of guilt fills Megan at having forgotten the easiest solution. "Should I call dad too?"

"Of course, but check in with Val first," says her mother. "She needs to hear from you. I'll call her in a minute so make it snappy. I need to hear her voice." The attempt at lightening her tone fails completely.

"What do I do?" Megan's whispered plea for direction barely stirs the heavy silence that has fallen between them.

"You be there for your classmates, love. I'll settle my people at the hospital as quickly as possible and meet you at Aunt Claire's as soon as I can. Be brave. I love you a hundred thousand times over."

After a few more rounds of love declarations and reassurances, Megan finally ends the call with her mother and dials her sister. Her heart climbs into her throat during the agonizing wait, but she's not terribly surprised Valerie doesn't answer. She usually has her phone on silent unless she's in the middle of a bathroom run. Finally, her sister's stupid voicemail greeting comes on.

"This is me! If you don't know who I am, then you've probably got the wrong gal. Say your piece and if I like you, I'll get back to you. Toodles!"

"Val, it's me, pick up!" says Megan. "Look, I need to know if you're all right. If you're messing with me on purpose, I'll kill you." She winces at the poor word choice, but forges on. "Please. Please, pick up. Mom says to go to Aunt Claire's when you can. She'll probably be at the hospital late tonight, but she says she'll meet us there. Call me the second you get this message. I hope you're safe. Please, be safe. I ... don't know what I'd do without you."

Upon ending the call to her sister, Megan sends her a lengthy text message with much the same sentiments. As she prepares to call her father, Megan glances around at her classmates. Every expression looks grim. Some quietly wipe at tears, but most simply draw shallow breaths and wait. Because it's an Italian class, the age range is wider than many other courses.

Two sophomore girls cling to each other next to Megan. They shiver with fear. One has light hair and one has dark hair. For some reason, they remind Megan of Val and her best friend, Sherri Colt. Moved by the sight, Megan shifts so she's between the younger girls and drapes her arms over their shoulders. She still wants to call her father, but a short delay won't make that much difference in the long run. For the first time, Megan begins to understand her mother's need to help others during a crisis.

Chapter 31:
Tense Situation

Monday, 2:51 p.m.
Brantford Regional High School
Brantford Township, New Jersey

"Kiernan! Here! Now!"

Officer Bonnie Kiernan's back automatically stiffens as Captain Grant Rischer barks her name. The man typically only has one tone, which can be described as demanding, but he sounds especially agitated today. She jogs over, trying hard not to picture herself as her dog, Peanut, answering a summons.

"I advise against this, sir," says Lieutenant Meredith Cooper.

"Noted," replies Captain Rischer, before turning to Bonnie. "Gear up. You're going in."

"We should wait until Dawson gets here," says Lieutenant Cooper. "I called him a half-hour ago. He should be here in twenty minutes."

"We might not *have* twenty minutes." Rischer's tone softens a hair as he lowers his voice to avoid the many curious ears turned his way.

"Where do you need me, sir?" asks Bonnie.

"Grab a headset and some burner phones from Kale and get to the school's main entrance ASAP," orders Rischer. "Vickers or Locke should be there to escort you to the media center. I'll explain as you run. Check in when the headset's in place."

Bonnie barely has the wits to nod thanks to Officer Kale who hands her two styles of headsets and three burner phones. Josiah Dawson has the most hours of training logged as a hostage negotiator, but he's half a state away at a conference on the latest and greatest techniques to diffusing tense situations. By comparison, Bonnie's just started on the journey. Still, she's here and he's not, so the job falls to her. The burner phones feel like ten-pound weights in her pocket.

Donning the slimmer headset, Bonnie checks in to make sure the thing works before leaving Kale's side.

"Good luck," Kale mouths when everything checks out.

Bonnie gives him a tight smile before running down to the road. She instinctively checks both directions. Traffic's nonexistent because some of her colleagues have blocked off the road to anything but emergency personnel. Once safely across, she sprints toward the school's main entrance.

Her boss's voice speaks in her ear just as she passes the midway point of the front lawn.

"Sorry we don't know much." The captain's voice is gruff, like he's not used to apologizing. "I'm getting conflicting stories from in there. The one thing they agree on is that there's a hostage situation going down either in or near the media center. Stay sharp and report back as soon as you know anything. Transmit everything if you can manage it."

"Yes, sir." Bonnie winces, but she silently admits that the captain's request falls in the reasonable category. Fair or not, until somebody of a higher rank shows up, everything that happens from here on out will be credited—or blamed—on the captain.

Officer Corey Vickers meets her at the first set of glass doors and holds one open for her.

"Right this way, ma'am," says Vickers.

Bonnie knows him from their brief, passing conversations near the coffee maker, but that's about it.

Vickers strides quickly down the deserted hallway and takes the first left.

"What can you tell me?" Bonnie inquires, jogging to keep up.

"Nothing," answers Vickers. "Sarge might know more. He's the one who had the captain ask for you."

Will I need my gun?

The thought worries Bonnie. She's never so much as pulled her gun in a real situation, let alone fired it. To her knowledge very few on the force have ever needed to discharge their service weapons on duty.

Last year, Nolan Locke had to kill an aggressive five-point buck that had somehow gotten inside an enclosed backyard and refused to leave, but that's about it.

"This is your stop. You'll do great," Vickers whispers. His tone carries a farewell with it. "Media center's down on the left."

"Where are you going?" Bonnie wonders. She peeks around the corner and spots Sergeant Gaits waiting tensely with his back to them.

"Locke and I are going to sweep the building for other threats," says Vickers.

"That's a big job," Bonnie notes.

Vickers shrugs.

"Campers and Skillman are already taking the upstairs. It should be done soon."

"Good because I know the EMTs are chomping at the bit to get in here," says Bonnie. Her mind immediately goes to her friend, Wendy Freeman, who'd cornered her soon after arriving on the scene with three other members of the volunteer squad. "Will we need them?"

"Definitely."

The surety in Vickers's voice and the sad look in his dark eyes chill Bonnie. She follows his gaze over to a darkened room with the door ajar. A pair of legs stick out from the doorway. Her breath catches in her throat and she takes a step toward the fallen figure before Vickers catches her arm.

"He's fine. Sarge is waiting for you." Vickers's features have gone stony. "Sooner the crisis ends, the sooner we can get him help."

"Who is it?" Bonnie can't help asking the question.

"Sean Burgess." Vickers gently turns her around and nudges her toward Sergeant Gaits.

Bonnie's heart sinks to her toes. A mental image of the affable officer and his family comes to mind. She's only met his wife and children once, but one would have to try very hard to forget Jennifer Burgess. The woman's fiery red hair had passed on untainted to both the boy and the girl.

A shout followed by a gunshot pulls Bonnie's attention back to the current situation.

A half-dozen quick steps brings her to Sergeant Gaits's side. He is tucked into a small alcove created by a set of double doors leading out to a courtyard holding a fountain. Another set of double doors goes to an enclosed courtyard featuring several trees and bushes.

"I'm here," Bonnie announces, kneeling beside the sergeant.

"What can I do?"

"Ian? Are you still there? Stop firing the gun. Do you hear me? Stop it!" Sergeant Gaits shouts toward a closed door ahead and to their left.

"I'm done talking!" The shout is distinct but faint through the bullet holes in the closed door.

"We're here to help." Bonnie raises her voice so that it carries through the door. "But it would be a whole lot easier if we could talk by phone. This is Officer Bonnie Kiernan with the Brantford Township Police Department. Will you let me give you a phone? Please."

A few beats of silence pass.

"There's nothing to say." This statement is softer. "The door's locked anyway."

"It's just glass. I can deal with that if you let me," says Bonnie.

"No. You'll rush in and kill me." The male voice sounds weary.

"I'm not here for that," Bonnie promises. "I just want to get everyone home safe. It's been a long day."

The voice chuckles darkly.

"It'll be longer still if I have my way."

"What do you mean by that?" Bonnie works very hard to modulate her voice.

Show no fear.

"You'll see," says Ian.

"Sometimes, people need things explained for them, Ian," says Bonnie. "Can I please just give you a phone so we can talk without shouting through a wall?"

Silence answers her.

Sergeant Gaits opens his mouth to say something, but Bonnie shakes her head and waves for him to be patient.

"Leave it by the door. I'll have somebody pick it up." The voice sounds cold and dead.

Bonnie moves to stand but Gaits catches her arm.

"Give me the phone," he orders.

"No." Bonnie shocks herself and the sergeant with the refusal.

"I not letting you get shot on my watch," he says, keeping his voice low so it won't carry through the bullet holes.

"Sir, if he sees you, he probably will shoot," Bonnie reasons, gently pulling free.

"Slide it into position then," says Gaits, "because you're not going out there."

Bonnie nods. It's only a few feet anyway. Laying one of the phones on the ground, she gives it a gentle shove toward the door. It hits but then slides along the door and out of reach of somebody opening the door. Taking out a second phone, Bonnie repeats the sliding motion but aims further left. This one lands near the opening within easy reach.

"The phone's ready for pickup!" she calls through the door.

They wait with their gazes fixed on the phone.

A moment later, the door slides open a few inches and an arm reaches out to pick up the phone. Then, the arm disappears with the phone leaving the door slightly ajar.

Sighing with relief, Bonnie checks in with her boss outside.

"The phone's been delivered. It's phone two," she reports.

"Good work. Call the number. Try to find out how many hostages he has and where they are in the room. We're working on getting equipment for that but it could be a while before it arrives. Keep everybody alive in there."

The affirmative response gets stuck in Bonnie's throat, but she manages to force it out.

"Yes, sir."

Chapter 32:
The Bell

Monday, 2:55 p.m.
Brantford Regional High School
Brantford Township, New Jersey

A student yelps, startling everybody. Still cooped up in the prep room, Naomi flinches with the rest of the crowd. She can't even tell if a guy or a girl spoke.

"Sorry!" says the student, definitely a girl. "My phone works!"

Her announcement electrifies the whole class.

Naomi and Alycia exchange panicked looks. If they don't do something instantly, the noise level will skyrocket. Although still convinced their part in the terrible day must be done, they can't risk drawing the wrong attention back to this room.

Naomi's back support shifts as Joey moves, but she catches her balance.

"Wait! Let me call 911 first. Then, everybody can make their calls," says Naomi.

"No speaker phone," Alycia adds to the students. "We still need to be quiet." She meets Naomi's questioning gaze. "Except the first call. I think we all need to hear that."

Agreeing, Naomi presses the digits for emergency services.

Somebody picks up almost instantly.

"911. This is Anton. What is your emergency?" The young man's voice sounds tense and excited.

"I'm at Brantford Regional High School. There's been a shooting," answers Naomi.

Probably multiple shootings.

"What is your name?" asks Anton. "Where are you located? And are there others with you?"

"My name is Naomi Harrison-Kensley, and I'm here with a friend, Alycia Teller, and her class. We're in the prep room between rooms 104 and 106. They should be able to tell where that is from the outside because there are numbers on some of the windows."

"Thank you, ma'am. That information will be very helpful. Officers are already on scene. How many students are with you?"

Naomi looks at Alycia for an answer.

"Twenty-two," Alycia says.

"Is anybody injured?" asks the emergency operator.

"No," says Naomi.

"Yes," answers Alycia at the same moment. She glares at Naomi.

"It's not bad," Naomi quickly explains. "I got grazed by a bullet. We're just grateful to be alive."

"Where were you injured, ma'am?" asks Anton.

"Back of my neck," Naomi answers. "Like I said, it's just a graze. I'll be fine."

"I'll make a note of it along with your location," Anton promises. "That should move you up the priority list. Sit tight. I need to transfer you to field another call, but I think you should speak with an officer."

Before Naomi can answer, a new man comes on the line.

"Captain Rischer, Brantford PD. What can I do for you?"

Naomi repeats much of the conversation she had with the 911 operator. The captain thanks her for the details and promises to relay the information to his people.

He transfers her to the lieutenant coordinating the officers inside. Meredith Cooper's voice is cold as ice, but Naomi finds her brisk efficiency comforting.

"We actually have—"

The rest of the officer's words get cut off by the bell ending the school day.

Naomi watches as several students instinctively start to rise. She waves them back down. It's heartbreaking to watch the relief change to confusion, dejection, and strain again.

Just a little longer.

"I'm sorry, I missed your last statement," says Naomi. "Can you please repeat that?"

"I said we have several officers near your location, but I'm going to need you to stay put. When it's safe, I'll send people to escort you out."

"Promise?" asks Hope.

"I promise," says the lieutenant. The woman's voice softens as she addresses them. "I've got a lot of good people coming. We'll have you out as soon as possible."

With nothing else to say, Naomi and the officer exchange a few more reassurances.

After ending the call, Naomi looks up to find every eye upon her.

"We should make a break for it," says Joey. He leaps to his feet. "Oh wow! Look at all the cops and—"

"Get down!" Alycia orders. She shifts to a position where she can tackle the kid if necessary.

Being closer but still not wishing to move her neck much, Naomi reaches back and blindly swats at the kid's leg.

"You heard her," she says. "Stay down."

"But I want to watch," Joey protests.

"You want to get shot?" demands another boy.

"Make your phone calls." Alycia moves her gaze around the room to convey the suggestion to everybody.

"Can't," says Joey. "Phone's dead."

"I'm sure someone will let you borrow their phone when they're done," Naomi says. "Meanwhile, come sit with me." She pats the ground next to her. "Or take up the post you abandoned behind me."

"Oh, sorry." Joey quickly sits down behind her again.

"Ah, that's better. Thanks." Naomi's certain she could manage sitting upright on her own now, but she also doesn't mind giving Joey something to do. If it keeps him seated, she's all for it.

For a time, Naomi lets the low murmur of conversations wash over her. She contemplates calling Jack, but doesn't want to disturb him. He's probably just finishing a long day of meetings.

Are you stupid? You could have died today. You could still die today. Call the man!

Blunt as always, her inner voice clears up the hesitation.

Scrolling over to her note, Naomi sends it with a brief addition that she's going to call now too. A few taps and she has Jack's number primed and ready to go.

After four rings, his voicemail picks up.

"Hey there…" Naomi scrambles frantically for something to say. "I … just sent you a cryptic note. Didn't want it to scare you too badly. Do me a favor. Don't watch the news. It'll only drive you crazy. I'll be all right. Love you. Oh, and don't worry if I'm out of touch. It's going to be a long night here. I'll call again when I can."

Chapter 33:
Tough Calls

Monday, 3:00 p.m.
Brantford Regional High School
Brantford Township, New Jersey

After hanging up with one of the science teachers, Lieutenant Meredith Cooper continues staring in the general direction of her phone. Head bowed and eyes closed, she futilely wishes the day away. She's got half a dozen largely untested officers running around a school turned war zone and one wounded officer probably bleeding out while the higher ups dither. So much help has come in that they're starting to get in each other's way. To make matters worse, the captain's deep in conference with the mayor, leaving her no one handy to pass the responsibility onward and upward.

The sun's warmth feels good across her shoulders, combatting some of the chilly wind. Part of her feels guilty being able to enjoy anything while her people face danger. If she didn't think Captain Rischer would have a heart attack on her, she'd charge right into the building to be with her children. She never calls them such because she has the aloof aura of "ice queen" to maintain, but the thought of losing any of them makes her queasy.

"Excuse me, ma'am, but is there any word on when we'll be able to get inside?" The speaker, a mid-forties man with a receding hairline, keeps a respectful distance as he addresses her. "I've got six crews standing by and three more enroute."

"You'll know when I know, O'Connor," says Meredith, instinctively reading the guy's name on his shirt.

"All due respect, ma'am. That's not good enough." O'Connor takes a half-step forward and lowers his voice. "We've got reports of wounded and dead in three separate classrooms. We can save the wounded, but every second's delay risks their lives."

"Which classrooms?" Meredith fires the question like an interrogation volley.

O'Connor fumbles in his pocket for a piece of scrap paper, looks at it briefly, flips it around, then rattles off a few numbers. "204, 206, 105, and 103."

"Add 106 and 104 to your list," says Meredith. "There's one more person wounded inside the prep room, and one of my officers is somewhere in that vicinity. He's been shot in the leg."

"Yes, ma'am. May I move my people into position to enter?" asks O'Connor.

She hesitates. To her knowledge, no gunshots have come through the front of the school. Still, the last thing Meredith needs is having the help taken out by stray bullets. She could order the SWAT guys to protect them, but the EMTs will likely become spread out and SWAT still needs to keep clearing the school. Even the rumor of bombs must be taken seriously.

"I can't spare officers to protect your crews yet, so if you move forward, stay flat on the ground."

O'Connor turns to sprint away.

"I mean it. Flat." Meredith pauses a second to drill the instruction into the EMT. "And keep your radios tuned to Emergency Talk Group 23. I'll give the go as soon as I can."

Nodding vigorously, the EMT rushes away.

Accessing her radio, Meredith orders her people to check in.

Kiernan and Gaits report no change. The suspect still has several hostages in a room off from the media center, but they managed to give him a phone. Vickers and Locke have cleared half the first floor of the school without finding any bombs, but they still have quite a bit of ground to cover. Campers and Skillman finished scanning the upper floor to catalog places to send EMTs, but need to do a second round for possible threats.

"Vickers. Locke. See if Gaits needs help," says Meredith. "I'll send new crews in to clear the rest of the first floor. We need to speed this up."

Barely registering acknowledgement from both officers, Meredith contemplates the situation. On the one hand, her crew is stretched very thin and several others stand ready, willing, and able to help. On the other hand, this isn't a training session with rubber bullets. If she mixed in too many unfamiliar crews with jittery nerves, somebody could die by friendly fire. As despair starts creeping in, the simple solution pops into her head.

Scrolling through her recent calls, she pulls up Captain Winston Phillips's number and contacts him. He answers midway through the first ring.

"Phillips," he says tensely.

"I thought of a use for your people."

"Excellent. How can we help?" Relief fills each word.

"Pair up an officer with each EMT crew and get people to every entrance and each room where shots were fired. When we can get the evacuation flowing, I want it to run as smoothly as possible. Do you have enough officers?"

"Not personally, but we should between Hamill, Narwick, and myself," Phillips assures her. "I'll take point on coordinating that, unless you want to do the honors."

"No, that's fine. You know the officers better than I do. Thanks." Ending the call, Meredith clenches and unclenches her left fist to relieve some of the nervous energy. Everything in her wishes to be inside having a chat with the little troublemaker who launched this mess.

Another thought occurs to her. How will they organize who goes to which hospital and who gets to go first? The EMTs can likely categorize people based on need, but the earlier reports from the patrols she sent out tell her that the need will still far outstrip the available aid.

Calling Phillips back, Meredith explains her new concerns.

"How many people can you spare?" she asks.

"None. Why?" Phillips wonders.

"Because we need to expand our roadblocks," Meredith says.

"Won't that make matters worse?" inquires Phillips.

"We need to keep the roads clear for emergency crews to exit in several directions. I want Englewood, Hackensack, Valley, and St. Joseph's all notified and placed on high alert."

"Already done," Phillips says calmly. "Two helicopters are on the way, where should I send them when they arrive?"

"I guess the softball and football fields," replies Meredith. "They're the only places I can see having enough room right now. All the parking lots are full."

"That was my thought, but I figured I'd confirm," says Phillips. "I already have most exits covered. I'll have a few of the sides streets turned into parking for parents to keep them off the main paths. Anything else you can think of? Closter, Emerson, Alpine, and Englewood police should arrive soon."

"I think we have enough bodies in play on site here," says Meredith, eyeing the beehive of activity around her. "But get them to spread out and pave the way for ambulances to access the Garden State Parkway and the other roads that lead to the hospitals."

Meredith's phone beeps to let her know she has a second call. Having little else to cover with Phillips, she conveys more thanks and switches over to Gaits's call. Usually the Sergeant would contact her via the radio, but there's a good chance he already tried that and got ignored during her focused conversations with Phillips.

"How's our girl doing?" Meredith asks.

"Fine." Gaits's tone indicates otherwise. "I think she's starting to get through to him."

"Then why do you sound tense?" Meredith wonders.

"Chatter tells me you're going to breach soon," says Gaits.

"Probably true," Meredith says. "The final pieces are being placed as we speak."

"You can't begin the evacuation yet!" Gaits speaks quickly. "If this kid gets wind of it, everybody in that room is dead."

"I … can't make any promises, but I'll take your thoughts under advisement." Meredith's heart does triple time within her chest. She extricates herself from the conversation as swiftly as possible, but her mind is already searching viable paths.

Which way will save the most lives? Evacuating the entire school simultaneously will mean this whole ordeal ends sooner and ultimately get the wounded to hospitals much sooner. A quiet evacuation will be much slower. Can the students and teachers be trusted to keep silent to even pull off a hushed evacuation? Knowing human nature, Meredith knows the answer to that. No. Inevitably some selfish kid—or teacher—will forget or ignore an order to be quiet. Either call has the potential to save people and get them killed.

"Lieutenant? This is Sergeant Dan Vole, Ridgewood PD. All officers have their assignments. Captain Phillips said the final go ahead would come from you. May we breach?"

If she had the time, Meredith could run a proper pros/cons

analysis, but she's out of time.

"Soon, sergeant, but I need you to get a message to everyone first. Begin the evacuation with the rooms on the left half of the school and the extreme right half of the school. Tell the entire middle to sit tight, especially those on the upper floors. Absolutely no change can be detected. There's a hostage negotiation going on in the media center and nothing can disturb that. It's a very dicey situation."

"Understood. Give me a minute to convey that through the group channel, and I'll check in again." Vole stops speaking for two seconds. "Then again, it might be better coming from you. Hang on. I can patch you through." A brief burst of static floods the radio speaker before settling down to charged silence. "Go ahead, ma'am."

As much as she wants to skip to the main point, the weight of the moment strikes Meredith. She doesn't even know how many ears she'll reach, but every word will be analyzed later.

"Thank you all for helping today. It's a dark day for this town and it's not over yet, but it's inspiring to see everyone rise to the occasion. There's still an active situation in the center of the school, but we need to start evacuating students and teachers as quickly and quietly as possible starting with the extreme left and right, ground floor first. I cannot stress the importance of silence enough, especially near the media center. Instead of using the school's PA system, you'll be clearing the rooms one by one. Deactivate the fire alarms if you use emergency exits. Get the students out and across the street ASAP, but take the time to let them know they must exit quietly. If you have any questions, speak now. There are no re-dos on this. We get this right and save lives. Period." Meredith pauses to allow for possible questions. Hearing nothing, she takes a deep breath. "Begin the evacuation."

Chapter 34:
The Swarm

Monday, 3:05 p.m.
Parking Lot of St. Mary's Church
Brantford Township, New Jersey

The scene unfolding before Faith Moffitt breaks her heart. Like a glimpse into a dystopian future, groups of students file out of the building from every exit, hands held high. They walk past the watchful gazes of dozens of armed police officers. Knowing the officers are genuinely there to help does not remove the sense of foreboding from the sight.

A few students gingerly step across the flat roofs to the front left corner where the fire department has erected a ladder. Most do not have their backpacks, but those that do are directed into the center lawn where they empty the contents of their bags onto the grass before throwing down the empty containers. Then, they continue the journey across the lawn and the road to the expansive parking lot spreading out behind Faith.

Her vision blurs with tears. She can't put words to the horror and helplessness. She can barely maintain her balance and continue scanning the crowd incessantly until she spots her son's familiar face. Rushing over, she sweeps him into a huge hug. A small crowd of students forms a pocket around them. For a precious moment, Faith forgets everything but the bliss of having found her son.

All too soon, Lucas tries to pull away.

"Mom! We're in public." He speaks low, so his friends won't hear him.

The boy standing a step behind Lucas comments anyway.

"It's cool, man, if my mom were here, I'd let her hug me. Ya have to after the sh—uh, the stuff that went down."

Still clinging to Lucas, Faith turns until she can see the speaker.

"I'm glad you're safe, Marik," says Faith. Reaching out with her left arm, she invites the boy into a hug.

Soon, she has six or seven students drawn into one big group hug. The crowd shifts and Lucas follows his classmates up to the main building to make room for more students and teachers to evacuate into the parking lot.

Faith returns to watching the exodus. When the sight becomes too painful, her eyes go up to the cheerful blue sky. The peace and beauty there doesn't match her feelings until her gaze flicks over to the line of bare trees. There, amidst the stark barrenness and sharp branches, Faith finds something that matches her emotions.

She tries to pray but no words form in her head or her heart. The only comfort she has is knowing Lucas made it out safely. So many questions remain about colleagues and friends.

"Would you like to help?" A gentle touch accompanies the question.

Faith flinches and whirls to face a smiling woman wearing a dark blue uniform. The lady's bright red hair barely stays confined to a messy bun at the back of her head. A smattering of freckles goes well with her smile. Faith might have slapped the lady on principle if it wasn't immediately apparent that the smile held no mirth, just kindness. The stitching above the woman's right breast pocket reads Freeman.

"With what?" Faith's return question is harsh and cautious.

"Name's Wendy. I'm with the Brantford Township Volunteer Ambulance Services." The woman holds out a hand for Faith to shake but smoothly turns the move into a waving gesture a moment later. "One of my crew members just arrived with a couple of hundred water bottles. You look like you need something to do to keep you from going stir crazy. Would you like to help with the distribution?"

Faith manages a brief nod and lets Wendy lead the way over to a bright red SUV with all it's doors open. Several blue-clad men and women haul out cases of water and move them over to a thin strip of grass separating two areas of the parking lot.

"Here. This is a great spot. Most of the kids will pass right by this patch," says Wendy.

Automatically, Faith shakes her head.

"The main entrance is on the far side. This is the exit," she explains, pointing to indicate what she means. The front exit from the school feeds almost directly into the entrance to the church lot on the other side.

"I see. Thanks. I'll get some people posted over there too," Wendy promises. "You should stay here. Mingle. Do you know any of the students?"

"Some," Faith answers. "I mainly work at the middle school now, but I help out with the plays and teach an occasional class over here. My son is also here, but most of his friends have already been by."

"And your son?" inquires Wendy.

"I saw him," Faith says, relief apparent in her tone.

"Great. Well, all of the students probably just need to see a familiar face right now," says Wendy. "Do as much or as little as you can, but if you're feeling faint or just out of sorts, go take a break in one of the rigs. It's going to be a few minutes until we can get geared up for transporting anybody."

At first, the task of handing out water bottles proceeds awkwardly. Several students and teachers walk past Faith as if she doesn't exist. The blank expressions are even worse than the tear-streaked ones. When the rush dwindles down to a slow trickle, Faith picks up several water bottles and moves through the crowd looking for people to help. She's grateful to see tearful reunions happen.

When did all the parents get here? Where are they coming from?

She glances around in confusion until she sees a suited man step out of the trees lining the left side of the parking lot. The police must have directed parents to park on the side streets.

The man nervously tugs at the stiff collar and loosens his blue striped tie, frowning down at his phone. He lifts his head and eyes the crowd in dismay.

"Who are you looking for?" Faith's question startles the man. She shivers, trying to remember walking towards him.

"My daughter." His answer is short and clipped. "She's a freshman."

"Do you know what she had last period today?" Faith wonders.

"No. Why does that matter?" The man glares at Faith for a full second before the fire drains, leaving worry in its place.

138

"They've begun evacuating the school but only from certain sections," Faith says, only just coming to the realization.

"Dad!" calls a shrill female voice.

Every man looks around anxiously.

A tiny, blond figure darts out from the nearby crowd and slams into the suited man standing with Faith.

"You came!" cries the girl.

"Of course, I came." The man stands stiffly merely enduring the embrace for a second before sagging with relief. Unshed tears make his eyes shiny.

Faith slowly backs away to give them some time together.

"Thank you," says the man hoarsely.

Faith merely nods, aware she didn't do a blessed thing. On the way back to the dwindling case of water, Faith distributes the few bottles in her arms. An ache moves through her left forearm, but she ignores the discomfort. Her knees pop as she stands from reloading.

"Need a hand?" asks a woman.

"Sure," Faith nods down at the three remaining water bottles. "Grab those."

"Can I ask you some questions?" The woman's question warrants her a second glance. Her perfectly styled hair, bright smile, and manicured nails scream reporter. The white blouse, blue blazer, and sensible heels do the same.

Without answering the question, Faith goes about her business of finding the most miserable looking kids and handing each a bottle of water, so they have something to cling to while searching for loved ones.

"You're Faith Moffitt, right?" calls the reporter.

Surprise causes Faith to freeze.

"Sorry, I didn't mean to frighten you. I'm Rebecca Treddle, Channel 12 News, but you can call me Becca if you like. You're the one who called 911. Can I get a statement from you?"

For the first time, Faith notices a man hovering nearby with a very large camera hoisted up onto his left shoulder.

"What kind of statement?" asks Faith.

"Your actions today may have saved dozens if not hundreds of lives, how does that make you feel?" The reporter's voice inflections are characteristic to a live report and dripping with enthusiasm. She doesn't exactly shove a microphone in Faith's face, but she might as well have. The same emotions are evoked.

"Terrible," Faith mutters, staring hard at the cameraman.

"It might be too early for this," concludes the reporter, dropping her "live TV" voice. "Jerry, take five."

The cameraman nods, lowers his camera, and ambles a few steps away.

"Why do you feel terrible?" Becca asks softly. "You're a hero."

Faith meets Becca's steady blue eyes.

"Heroes are only needed when things go wrong, and today, things went very, very wrong. People shouldn't need to do this kind of saving. Our society should be better than this."

"Can I quote you on that?" asks Becca. "It's a beautiful statement that needs to be shared."

Faith only shrugs and walks away.

Chapter 35:
Two Paths

Monday, 3:06 p.m.
Brantford Regional High School
Brantford Township, New Jersey

Sudden weariness washes over Ian Colt. He starts to nod off but shakes himself awake. The female police officer is still babbling over the phone line. Ian stopped paying attention to her words a few minutes ago. He's tempted to mute her, but her voice soothes the hostages, which is a good thing for now. Their calm gives him a chance to think in peace.

Suicide or make the cops do it?

It's an old debate, but the moment of truth is at hand.

Suicide would be the surer road, but the cops would probably be more than happy to oblige at this point. Ian's not quite certain he wishes to let one of the cops play hero. It would be one last insult to steal that honor from them. Still, part of him can't stomach going out by his own hand like his father. Sherri doesn't know that part. She thinks it was a simple, tragic mistake because that's what Ian and their mother told her. But nobody accidentally swallows an entire bottle of oxycodone.

This is different. You're using bullets. You've done way more than he ever could.

The argument feels hollow. The quarrelsome side of Ian's brain fires back with the things his father accomplished that he never would. He got married, had kids, owned a house, and drove a motorcycle.

You could always surrender. Then, maybe someday you'd have a chance at

141

those things.

Several recent school shooters have chosen the trial road. There's something poetic in forcing the state to both prosecute and defend you. Still, prison doesn't sound very appealing. Ian has no delusions of being tougher, stronger, and meaner than the hardened criminals who spend their lives bouncing in and out of prisons.

Seeing the fallout from his actions has a certain appeal, but it also opens the way for pain. The whole point of today was casting off social constraints and waking the world up to life's cruelties.

I'm a messenger. I must finish this.

"What's wrong?" Anabelle Lin's voice breaks through Ian's thoughts.

The question draws a cynical laugh from him.

What's not wrong?

"A lot more than we can cover in the short time we have left," he says.

"Then give us more time." Anabelle leans back against one of the tables making up a wall of the little fort they'd created. "Nobody wants to rush you."

The other girl looks at Anabelle, silently pleading with her to keep quiet.

"Ian, are the others all right?" asks the female cop, returning to the same line of questions and demands like clockwork. "Send out the wounded so we can get them medical attention. You don't want them to die."

Apparently, ignoring her does nothing.

"Listen, lady. If I shot them, I want them to die, so why would I let you help them?" The anger gives him a tension headache.

The policewoman shushes him like a baby.

"Easy, Ian. Talk to me. Let me know what you want, and I'll work on it. I'm your friend—"

"You are *not* my friend," Ian retorts. "You're probably sitting with a dozen people who'd like nothing better than to come shoot me, so don't pretend we're friends."

"You need people on your side," says the cop.

"What I need is peace and quiet." Ian stares down at the loaded handgun. He doesn't have many bullets left, but one well-placed bullet is all it would take. "And there's only one way to get it."

"No! Think of your family, your friends, you have so much to live for." Desperation defines the officer's tone.

"I killed my sister," Ian says. His glare finds Anabelle's stricken face. He should probably tie her up again, something he forgot to do when she retrieved the phone for him. "She was the first."

The statement earns him a gasp and three full seconds of complete silence.

"Why?" The cop's question is so soft Ian almost misses it.

"I don't know," he answers honestly. "Because she deserved it."

"What was her name?" inquires the cop.

"Sheridan. Why does that matter?"

"How old was she?" asks the officer.

Anger fills Ian again.

"It doesn't matter. It's not about her. It never was. I killed her. That should be the end of it."

"People are going to wonder why," says the cop.

"I don't owe them anything." The statement has a freeing effect on Ian's emotions. "I'm tired of following nonsense rules and doing meaningless things. My life is finally going to mean something. Count the bodies. If it's more than seventeen, you're talking to a world record holder."

Silence answers him again.

"Are you impressed?"

"Horrified," says the cop.

"It's close. I'll take it," Ian says, suddenly in a good mood. "Now, if you'll excuse me, I have to end this. It's been fun. Remember me fondly."

For a third time, a lengthy silence falls.

"Aren't you going to try to stop me again?" Ian wonders.

"What's left to say?" returns the cop.

"You tell me. You had no trouble the first six times through this conversation," says Ian.

"I want to help you, but you have to meet me in the middle," says the cop, clearly frustrated.

"That's a little difficult to do with a wall and a few tables between us." The weariness returns with a vengeance. "I'd say this has been fun, but it hasn't. You're boring me."

Ian pokes the end call button with enough force to jam his finger. Looking up, he meets Anabelle's frightened eyes.

"No. No." The rest of her protests fade as her voice fails.

"Ladies first," says Ian, lifting the handgun and placing it gently on her forehead.

143

"Please don't kill me." Tears accompany the plea as Anabelle shrinks away from Ian. She looks so pathetic curled up in a ball, back pressed against one of the tables. "Please."

"Face me," Ian orders.

Anabelle clenches her eyes shut and shakes her head violently. The movement moves her whole body. She reaches back to stabilize herself and knocks into one of the table legs. Her hands fly out and clamp around the metal, clinging for dear life.

Ian watches the process, fascinated. His gun is now pointed at the side of her head.

"Face me!" Ian repeats.

"No!" This protest contains a lot more force than the last one. Anabelle's eyes remain firmly closed. "You don't always get what you want."

An explosive shout roars out of Ian. In two swift moves, he knocks his right elbow into the side of Anabelle's head then reverses direction and smacks her with the handgun. She crumples to the ground.

The violence surprises Ian. His hands start to shake. Needing something to do, he ejects the magazine and counts the bullets. It doesn't take him long. There's only one left in the clip. That plus the one seated in the chamber gives him a grand total of two bullets in that gun. The other one might have a half-dozen at best.

Now or never.

Closing his eyes, Ian presses the gun to his right temple.

Chapter 36:
I'll Guide You

Monday, 3:11 p.m.
Brantford Regional High School
Brantford Township, New Jersey

A knock brings Naomi's attention back to the present moment. She turns her head toward the door. The movement stretches her neck painfully, but she blinks and raises a finger to her lips. Everybody stops moving.

"This is Officer Ken Ramos of Emerson. The evacuation has begun. I'm here to escort you out of the school. May I come in?" The officer keeps his voice calm and even, like speaking too loudly would scare them off.

"Show us your badge," calls Naomi. "There's a small gap in the door. You can use that."

She doesn't care about seeing the badge, but she needs the time to verify that the evacuation has begun. For several minutes, they've been hearing faint movements around the building, but nobody dared to stand up and check. Slowly getting up, Naomi maneuvers to an area of the front window not obscured by too many boxes. Leaning forward, she lifts the shade enough to see students streaming out of the building.

"I wonder why they're so quiet," she murmurs.

"There's still an ongoing incident," answers Officer Ramos. He pushes on the door and gets stymied by the stack of textbooks.

Naomi and Alycia exchange questioning looks. Finally, Naomi

145

nods.

"Help me slide the textbooks back," she says.

Eager to escape, the students snap into action. Joey and another nearby student grab books from the top of the stack and hand them back. Alycia coordinates where the displaced books should be moved to. When only six books remain in the stack Naomi slides the whole thing back and steps in front of the door.

"Are you sure it's safe to move them?" Naomi asks.

"We have a safe path out," says the officer.

"Lead on then," says Naomi, noting that the policeman sort of dodged the question.

"First, I need to tell them something." Ramos's grim expression speaks volumes. "May I?" He gestures, indicating his desire to move past her into the room.

"Trust is in short supply. Say what you need to from the threshold," says Naomi.

"Fair enough," replies Ramos. He steps forward as Naomi retreats a half-step.

She's still poised to slam the door into the man if he poses a threat.

"We need to move you out through this room, but I also need to warn you that a wounded officer was lying across the doorway until we could get him help just a minute ago," Officer Ramos explains. "To avoid seeing anything unpleasant, I want you to form a line behind your teacher. Put your hands on the shoulders of the person in front of you as best you can and keep your eyes fixed between their shoulder blades. Step carefully exactly where you see them step."

Hands tentatively touch Naomi's shoulders.

"Alycia," says Naomi, waving her friend forward.

The crowd of students parts enough to let the other chemistry teacher forward.

"Get them to safety," Naomi whispers, leaning close so only Alycia can hear.

Alycia nods but casts a curious glance at Naomi.

Turning around, Naomi catches the hands of the bewildered student behind her and places them gently onto Alycia's shoulders. Slowly, the strange procession moves out of the destroyed prep room. As each student moves through the doorway, Naomi guides their hands up to the proper position. Finally, the last student passes Naomi.

"Keep your eyes forward and don't stop until you're safe," she says, placing her hands gently on the young man's shoulders.

A sniffle stops Naomi in her tracks. Releasing the boy, she returns to the prep room. Soon, she discovers the source. Hope sits under the first desk, partially obscured by one of the rolling chairs. Moving the chair, Naomi kneels before the frightened girl.

"Hey. Come on out of there. This is our golden chance," says Naomi.

Drawing her legs closer, Hope rocks back and forth.

"I can't."

"Why not?" asks Naomi. Holding her neck to peer down causes shooting pain to radiate from the wound, forcing Naomi to look up. "I thought you wanted to get out of here."

"I do!" cries Hope. "But I'm afraid of blood. If I see it, I'll faint. Then, I'll be stuck here forever."

"I won't let that happen," Naomi promises. "You can do this. I'll guide you. Let's get you clear of the obstacles in this room. Then, you can close your eyes and follow the sound of my voice."

"What if I trip and accidentally open my eyes?" asks Hope.

"As long as your head's up, you'll only be able to see me," answers Naomi. She lets the statement rest a few seconds before taking Hope's hands in hers. "You'll have to scoot forward or you'll bash your head when you try to stand. Come now, it's time for some fresh air."

Once Hope gains her feet, Naomi guides her through the maze of textbooks littering the floor. When they reach the threshold leading into room 104, Naomi brings the girl to a halt.

"Okay, we're in the clear," says Naomi. "Close your eyes and think of somewhere safe. You'll be back wherever that is in no time." Slowly, Naomi walks Hope through 104. Progress is slow because Naomi needs to hold on to both of Hope's hands and walk backwards. Light spills in from the hallway, but she keeps checking behind her so she doesn't trip.

Blood soaked paper towels line the floor in front of the door.

"Keep going. We're almost there," urges Naomi. "Big step now. The texture's about to change. Don't worry about it."

"What is it?" Hope squeaks the question as her right foot comes down on a wad of paper towel.

Releasing the girl's left hand, Naomi catches hold of her chin and keeps it tilted upward.

"Don't look down," says Naomi. "Just a few more steps. You can do it."

Shuffling backwards moves some of the bloody towels. Naomi stops to shake a persistent piece off.

A gunshot rings out.

Hope screams along with several others.

With a mighty heave, Naomi pulls Hope into the hallway and across the hall to the line of lockers. Pushing the girl down, Naomi kneels beside her and draws her into a hug. The need to get lower causes her to pivot to a sitting position. Hope's sobs get drowned out by running boots and shouted orders.

"Get these people out of here!" calls a male voice.

Eyes firmly shut, Naomi doesn't see the speaker, but she feels a tug on her arm just before a different male voice speaks.

"Please stand up. Let me help you."

Naomi blinks up at the clean shaven young officer.

"Help her," she says, pushing Hope up towards the policeman.

He instinctively catches hold of Hope's arms and steadies her.

Rolling to her right, Naomi comes to her knees and peeks around the corner into the hallway running perpendicular to the one she's in. A cluster of police officers buzz near the door to the Glass Lab computer room off the media center.

The officer stationed to keep people out of the hallway watches the spectacle, hand poised over his service weapon like a Western gunslinger.

A nameless sensation in Naomi's gut pulls her forward into the hallway. Not really trusting her legs or wanting to present a large target, she slowly crawls down toward the commotion.

"Hey!" The shout comes from the young officer holding on to Hope. "You can't go down there."

Taking that as her cue, Naomi gets her legs under her and covers the rest of the distance in a running crouch.

Chapter 37:
Caravan

"You need to see this."

"Where are you?" Wendy Freeman has never heard her partner sound so grim. Usually, she can rely on Adam Garner to crack a joke no matter what they find.

"204, but the room next door is just as bad. Take the middle stairs up and turn right. It's down on the left. You can't miss us. We're going to need more rigs. What's the ETA on the helicopter?"

"One's three minutes out and another is fifteen, why?" Wendy asks.

"Because my initial assessment says three from this room won't make it another half-hour without immediate hospital care."

Adam's words terrify Wendy. He's earned the nickname Grim Reaper by almost always being correct in his predictions.

How do I assign them?

As shift supervisor and the one with the most experience for the home team, Wendy knows that most of the tough decisions will fall to her. She trusts her people to make sound decisions, but any close calls will be her problem.

Calling another two teams to her side, Wendy leads the charge up the stairs Adam mentioned.

149

"Stabilize as many people on site as you can. Prioritize those who can be saved and prep the worst of these for immediate transport," Wendy instructs. These crews aren't hers, so she feels obligated to give them clear instructions. The fewer questions they have, the better for everybody.

Without waiting for acknowledgement, Wendy slips into room 204 and stops in her tracks. She's never seen so much destruction in one place. The front of the room is relatively clear, but the back wall bears countless bullet holes. Two of the desks have nearly been torn in half. Bodies litter the room. Pens, pencils, computers, backpacks, and other school supplies are everywhere. Some pieces of paper have been so finely shredded they look like confetti.

"Is anybody uninjured?" Wendy asks, directing the question to Adam.

One of the other EMTs, a young woman with medium brown hair wraps gauze around a girl's arm. The kid stares off into space.

"I don't know," answers the woman. "There are five beyond help and three barely hanging on."

"Then, why are you helping that one?" Wendy tries to keep condemnation out of her tone. Well-aware how that could be taken, she raises a hand and continues. "I'm sorry, that came out wrong. Thank you for helping." She doesn't know this woman, but she is grateful for her presence.

"Two of the critical have already been removed, but we're working our way back," Adam explains quietly. "Sometimes a quick patch job keeps them calm enough to move. We still haven't even reached the ones buried in the back corner."

"What's your name?" Wendy asks the new EMT even as she nods to acknowledge Adam's words.

"Miriam."

"When you're done there, see if you can move that student over to the less damaged corner," instructs Wendy.

"Can't they be evacuated?" asks Miriam. "This isn't exactly the best environment for them."

"Most of them are in shock or soon will be," Wendy explains. "We can't release them fully until they're medically cleared, but we also need to get to the rest of them." She waves toward the deeper destruction. Unhooking her radio microphone, Wendy pages Jonas. "Can you bring me a popup screen?"

"Good idea," Adam comments.

Miriam agrees and returns to her task.

They don't usually need to keep prying eyes away, but this time, separating those with minor and major injuries will minimize further mental anguish for the victims.

Working together, Adam, Miriam, and Wendy move most of the desks to the front of the room so they can reach more of the wounded. As quickly as they unearth living souls, the three rescue workers patch up any holes as best they can and get them prepped to be moved to one of the rigs. Soon, there's a backup of people waiting.

"Wendy, are you there?" squawks a voice over her radio. "We have a problem."

"I'm here, Rose. Go ahead," replies Wendy.

"We're running out of rigs," says Rose Donahue.

"Double them up," says Wendy.

"We did," answers Rose. "All but the first two. There are at least three separate action sites."

Wendy's mind races. Running out of rigs now means a lot of wounded will need to wait for a return trip. That could cost lives.

"Does the school have any vans?" Wendy inquires.

"I believe so," Rose says cautiously.

"They do. I've seen them." Wendy's words come out faster as the excitement takes over. "Get me somebody from the Board of Education and every warm body with a CDL."

"You probably don't need a commercial driver's license for the vans," says Rose. "Would buses help? It's the end of the school day, nearly every bus assigned to the high school is here. The police didn't know what to do with them, so they lined them up on a side street. Oh, I almost forgot. There's a bloodmobile over at the local library. Would that help?"

"Definitely," says Wendy. "Get me the highest-ranking police officer on scene and whoever's running that bloodmobile."

"What do you have in mind?" wonders Rose. "Maybe I can save you some time by handling the bloodmobile call myself."

"I need stretchers, strong bodies, nurses, teachers, and every spare officer you can get me," says Wendy. "Get those buses in gear with as many walking wounded as possible. Even if they don't have any visible injuries everybody in any of the action sites should be held until they're cleared by a hospital psychiatrist."

Eight phone calls later, Wendy has everything in place with most of the proper clearances. She's not entirely sure the Board of Education representative understood her plan, but he gave her verbal permission to ask for volunteers. Every single bus driver offered their services, but Wendy thought it best to only commission four buses on the first run, one for each of the main hospitals in the area. They might need the others to move the students to a third location to be reunited with their parents.

Coordinating through text messages with her friend, Officer Bonnie Kiernan, Wendy got the personal number for Captain Grant Rischer who immediately embraced her idea. The rest of her calls went to her main contacts at each of the area hospitals. They needed to brace for a flood of patients. Two of the hospitals already knew what to expect. Dominique Marquette asked about her two daughters, and Wendy promised to be on the lookout for them.

Before Wendy can slip away to oversee her forming caravan, Adam calls her over.

"What do you think?" he asks, looking troubled.

Wendy's practiced eyes travel the length of the body Adam presents her with. The girl is unconscious, but a very subtle rise and fall of her chest says there's still life in her.

"How is she even alive?" Wendy has witnessed miracles before, but this kid has five bullet wounds, three in her stomach, one in her left side, and one through her left arm. The ones on her side and arm don't appear too bad, but the stomach wounds have leaked so much blood Wendy's surprised the girl has any left in her.

"Not all the blood is hers," says Adam. "Another girl's body was on top of her," Adam explains, pointing to a body laid out carefully on the floor. "I think the pressure kept blood loss to a minimum. I've done what I can, but she's soaking the pressure bandages almost as quickly as I can place them. What do I do? Should I ...."

"Yes, try to save her," says Wendy. Searching around, she spots a wall of English textbooks. "Fill a backpack with books and put that over the stomach wounds. I'll direct the helicopter crew to come here. Looks like they have a customer." Her gaze flits back to the body Adam had pointed out, and she finally gets a good look at the girl's face. Tears spring to her eyes as realization crushes her.

She knows this girl.

It's Valerie Marquette.

What do I tell Dominique?

The question puts Wendy in a moral quandary. She should call Mrs. Marquette right away, but doing so will destroy her and potentially endanger more lives if the surgeon is not at the top of her game.

I'll tell her in person later. Wendy dreads the task, but she also won't leave this notification to others. Her friend deserves that much.

Chapter 38:
Weird Turn

Monday, 3:18 p.m.
Brantford Regional High School
Brantford Township, New Jersey

"Anything?" asks one of the older policemen.

He sounds like the man in charge, but Naomi's not about to inquire. She can still feel the baleful glare from the young man she dodged on her way into this section of hallway. Only uncertainty keeps him from outing her with a shout. She saw that much in his stance and expression.

"It's still ringing," says a young officer. She holds up a cell phone as if in proof before returning it to her ear. She has a headset, but it's looped around her neck.

Listening carefully, Naomi can make out an answering ring from inside the Glass Lab.

"He must be dead, right?" whispers a tall, male officer with dark skin.

Who's dead? Naomi's heart beats faster.

"Probably," answers yet another male officer. This one has pale skin and appears to be in his mid-twenties. "He threatened to do it like four times."

Ian? Naomi is not sure how to react to the possibility. On the one hand, if Ian is dead the threat might be over. Still, the relief that a young man might be dead sickens her.

"Should I continue, Sarge?" asks the officer with the phone.

"Yes, keep trying," says the sergeant. "I—"

He cuts himself off abruptly and levels a withering gaze at Naomi.

"What are you doing here?"

Naomi's cheeks flush as the four police officers stare at her.

"I came to help." Naomi cringes at the pathetic excuse.

The sergeant makes a noise that combines huff with snort and adds in a bit of a grunt. The tall policeman gives her a sympathetic look, while the shorter one shakes his head and returns his attention to the Glass Lab. The policewoman eyes Naomi coolly while attending to the task of re-calling the phone inside the room.

"Vickers, get this woman out—"

"Someone picked up!" The policewoman's excited whisper cuts off the sergeant. "Hello? Can you hear me? It's all right. Calm down." She shifts to lean against the wall, giving Naomi a chance to see her last name: KIERNAN.

"What's the matter?" demands the sergeant. Now that he's fully facing Naomi, she can read his nameplate which says: GAITS.

"She's hysterical, sir," reports the female officer.

"Let me try," says Naomi.

The police officers look at her doubtfully.

"This is Carlton Wright's social studies class," Naomi explains. "I've had most of the students in classes before, and I have a few of them currently. The girl on the line might recognize my voice."

The sergeant's glare turns thoughtful.

"You may be on to something," he mutters. "Bonnie, give her the phone."

The female officer quickly wipes the phone down with her shirt and hands it to Naomi.

"Put it on speaker but turn the volume low," says Gaits. "Get her calm, then let us handle this."

Naomi nods to let Gaits know she understands her role. He moves into place next to her right ear while Officer Kiernan moves to her left side. Naomi holds the phone up near her mouth and starts speaking.

"Hello? Can you hear me? This is Mrs. Harrison-Kensley. I have some … help with me, but you need to let us know the situation in there. Will you talk to me?"

Heavy breathing and sobs answer Naomi. Encouraged by the

fact that they're slowing down, Naomi repeats her message a few more times until the sobs subside to sniffles.

"What's your name? Am I speaking with Jessie? Fiona? Anabelle?" Naomi pauses briefly at each name.

"Yes," says the girl.

The word also appears in text form on the screen.

"Anabelle, excellent. Talk to us. What's going on in there?" asks Naomi.

A strange, high-pitched wail startles Naomi. She almost drops the phone, but Sergeant Gaits steadies her hand. Reaching over, he pokes a button to temporarily mute outgoing sounds.

"Ask her if we can come in," says Sergeant Gaits. He nods and the two male officers move into position to be able to enter the room swiftly.

After a few breaths to steady her nerves, Naomi pokes the same button Gaits did and speaks.

"It's okay. Don't think about it. Listen, we need to know if it's safe to come in. Is the danger ... gone?"

"He's dead." Anabelle's voice lacks emotion.

This time, Officer Kiernan presses the button to mute outgoing noises.

"Ask if she's safe," whispers Officer Kiernan. "We need to know where the weapons are."

Naomi dutifully repeats the question.

"Yes, I have his gun," says Anabelle.

A new fear stabs Naomi in the chest. She exchanges alarmed looks with both the negotiator and the sergeant.

"Anabelle, put the gun down," says Naomi.

"No. It will keep me safe," replies the girl.

"My friends will protect you, but you have to—"

"Are you safe?"

Anabelle's question blindsides Naomi.

"What? Of course, I am." Her mind scrambles to understand the child's leap of logic.

"Show me. Come in alone," says Anabelle.

Gaits presses the mute button.

"Absolutely not," he says. "There's no way I'm letting you out of my sight."

"She's just scared." Naomi knows she's waging a losing battle, but she feels obligated to try.

"But is she alone?" asks Officer Kiernan. The policewoman's expression is hard to read.

"What do you mean?" Naomi fires back, not exactly ready for mental gymnastics.

"What's on your mind?" Gaits directs the question to Officer Kiernan.

"That was a weird turn," mutters Vickers.

"Exactly," Officer Kiernan confirms. "Scared kids don't act like that … unless they're being fed the words."

"You think the kid's alive?" The sergeant's inflection makes it a question.

"Yes, sir," replies Officer Kiernan. "What should we do?"

"Is there any way to turn on the camera feature remotely?" The question comes from Vickers.

"Maybe," answers the shorter officer thoughtfully. His nameplate reads: LOCKE. "But you'd need a phone or a computer with the right software."

"Try to get the girl to come out," instructs Gaits.

"Anabelle, leave the gun there and come on out. We can protect you better out here," Naomi says.

"Help!" The girl's cry turns into a scream, followed quickly by a slapping noise and silence. A few seconds later, whimpered words can be heard. "I don't want to die."

"I'll second that for now. Let's play a game. What do you say HK? Thought I'd killed you before. Want to play with us?" The new voice is young, vibrant, and full of malice. "I don't have a revolver so it'll be a little difficult to play Russian roulette properly, but I'm pretty sure one of my handguns is out of ammunition. It'll be fun."

"Ian," Naomi breathes his name hoarsely. Unshed tears sting her eyes. "Don't do this."

"I'd rather play with you than Anabelle," Ian continues conversationally. "She's been crying so much, she probably won't even get what's happening."

Before Naomi can even consider Ian's request, the phone gets snatched away and her arms are pulled behind her back. Cold handcuffs slide into place and snap closed with ominous little clicking noises.

Sergeant Gaits puts a hand on her left shoulder to steady her.

"This is for your own good, ma'am."

Chapter 39:
My Turn

Monday, 3:25 p.m.
Brantford Regional High School
Brantford Township, New Jersey

We're gonna get sued.

Nevertheless, Officer Bonnie Kiernan has never agreed with Sergeant Gaits more. She pulls the teacher up and tugs backwards to get her to retreat. The handcuffs might be extreme, but people rarely move much when restrained. Not moving much might just save this woman's life, so it will be worth a few hard questions later if it comes to that.

"Your turn." The Crazy Kid's voice comes clearly through the phone's speakers.

"Get in there," snaps Gaits.

Vickers silently counts down from three to nothing, using his fingers so the others can follow.

"It's your lucky day," says Crazy Kid. "My turn."

As Vickers reaches zero, he yanks on the door handle. For one awful second, Bonnie fears the door is still locked. It is, but it still swings wide, having never completely shut after the girl retrieved the phone.

Not having time to retreat further, Bonnie presses the teacher against the wall and pushes down on her shoulders to force her to kneel. Then, she maneuvers around her to offer the meager protection of her bulletproof vest. Instinct causes her to draw her gun, but she keeps it pointed at the ground. Her job is to protect the teacher and provide

158

backup for Gaits, Vickers, and Locke.

Four gunshots crack through the air almost as one.

Springing to her feet, Bonnie rushes over to doorway and peers inside. At first, she doesn't see anything, but then, she spots her two colleagues and Sergeant Gaits spread out at three points of the room.

Each man looks grim.

The teacher squeezes in behind Bonnie who barely has the wherewithal to grab her arm and prevent her from moving further into the room.

"Ian?" calls the teacher. Her voice wavers with fear. "Anabelle?"

Sergeant Gaits pierces Bonnie with a displeased look. His eyes flick over to the door, but Bonnie pretends not to notice. Instead, she sidesteps in front of the teacher, keeping her gun at the ready in case something threatening pops up from behind the tables that have been turned onto their sides over in the far-right corner.

Tension spreads throughout the room.

Vickers, who has the middle position, steps closer to the corner. The others are a half-step behind him.

Bonnie's left boot taps as she tamps down on the urge to race forward and see what happened. She unconsciously holds her breath.

Vickers mutters something Bonnie can't quite make out. She hears Gaits's curse loud and clear. At a gesture from the sergeant, Vickers and Locke holster their weapons and each grip a side of the front table.

Like an insect seeking light in a fire, Bonnie moves further into the room so she can see. She keeps her arms spread to either side to keep the teacher back. They move into a location with a clear view just as Locke leans down and touches the arm of a huddled figure.

A piercing scream straightens Locke up instantly. He leans back and holds his hands out in front of his body in a futile attempt to ward off the continued screams. Vickers and Gaits take turns attempting to stem the tide of noise. Eventually, the howling screams subside into body-wracking sobs.

"Ma'am? Are you okay with the sight of blood?" Sergeant Gaits shouts to be heard.

"I'm fine," answers the teacher.

"Bonnie, set her loose. She needs to calm this kid down," says Gaits.

Relieved, Bonnie puts her gun away, slips the handcuffs off the teacher, and guides her forward. Vickers and Locke maneuver a table between several bodies but not before she glimpses the Crazy Kid. The sight turns her stomach, causing bile to burn the back of her throat. She counts three bullet wounds in the center of his body, one in each shoulder and one right over the sternum. Those must be from her colleagues. The fourth wound went straight into his brain. Bonnie's last glimpse of a wound like this was a forensic science class in college.

Trying to erase the sight from her mind, Bonnie kneels next to the teacher who tries to catch the Asian girl's attention without touching her.

"Hey, Sarge, I think some of these kids are alive!" Vickers's voice floats over the table. "Kid must have knocked them senseless before offing himself."

"Not this one," says Locke.

"See if you can carry them out before they wake up." Gaits sounds weary.

"It's over," says the teacher.

Even though the words are meant for the girl, Bonnie silently clings to them. She quickly loses track of the times the lady repeats the reassurance. Each iteration sinks the message in a little deeper.

"Try to get her to let us lead her out of this room," Bonnie urges. Only with effort can she keep her gaze on the girl.

A large bruise covers the whole left side of the child's face. Blood trickles down from a gash across her forehead. More blood—probably not hers—covers her clothes in speckles and streaks. Spotting a large gray sweatshirt lying next to a man's body, Bonnie checks the thing for blood and wordlessly offers it to the teacher.

"Anabelle. Some sad things happened here," explains the teacher. She drapes the sweatshirt across the girl's chest like a blanket. "We should move away from it. My friend and I want to take you somewhere you'll be … happier. We need to get you cleaned up and find your parents."

A tiny spark of something enters the girl's eyes at the mention of parents.

"Do you have their number, Anabelle?" asks Bonnie, taking her tonal cues from the teacher. "I'm a police officer. I can call them and let them know where to find you."

The girl only blinks in response.

Having a goal to aim for, Bonnie takes a few steps away and calls her reporter friend Becca Treddle and sends the woman to hunt up the kid's parents.

"What's her last name?" Becca wonders.

"Not sure," Bonnie admits. "Hang on."

Where would I find the girl's name?

She could ask the teacher, but that would require interrupting the impromptu therapy session. The other teacher would also know, but he's out of commission. Bonnie kneels beside him to check his pulse anyway, hoping she's the second person to do this. With the chaos, anything's possible. A clipboard near the man's body has a class roster. Bonnie scans down with her finger until she comes to Anabelle Lins. Thankfully, the class only has one student named Anabelle.

Bonnie reports the name to Becca.

"Do you think you can find the girl's parents?" Bonnie wonders.

"I can find anything," Becca says. "It would help if you could pull their number off Anabelle's phone, but I can get the info a different way. There's got to be a teacher around who has our girl on their roster. They'd have the information in a grading system."

"They're not just going to hand over that information," Bonnie points out.

"I'll just let them know that Officer Bonnie Kiernan is inquiring." A mischievous tone creeps into Becca's statement.

Bonnie gasps, gripping her phone so tightly it hurts.

"Relax," says Becca. "I'll keep it on the up and up today. Besides, you *are* seeking this information. Now, let me go. I have a job to do for you."

"Thanks, lady. I owe you," says Bonnie.

"Girl, how many times have I told you those are dangerous words to utter around a reporter?" asks Becca. "I think I found the exclusive interview I want to claim."

"We can discuss that later," Bonnie says, dodging the issue.

The possibility leaves an uneasy feeling in the pit of her stomach. She doesn't need to be clairvoyant to see the future. The next few weeks aren't going to be easy. Morbid curiosity will have everybody asking questions. Social media will buzz with stories, cries of outrage, pictures, memorials, and a thousand unsolicited opinions.

"Are you ready to go now?" The teacher's question isn't directed at Bonnie, but she silently answers it anyway.

More than ready.

Chapter 40:
What Happened?

Monday, 5:35 p.m.
Englewood Hospital and Medical Center
Englewood, New Jersey

"There you are. Why aren't you in a bed somewhere with a nurse yelling at you?" demands Alycia Teller.

"Because the beds are clearly going to be needed for others," replies Naomi Harrison-Kensley. She finishes signing her name on the release form before turning to her friend. "Besides, I've already been patched up." She turns her head slowly and sweeps her hair aside so Alycia can see the thick white bandage covering the entire back of her neck. "What are you doing here? Did you get hurt?"

"No, nothing like that," Alycia assures her. "Once we got outside, I found out they needed volunteers from the school to go with each batch of students being shipped out to the various hospitals. Luck of the draw brought me to this fanciness." She waves to encompass the overly cheerful hospital environment. "It's sheer madness back there. I needed to come up for air before returning." She gestures to one of the long hallways springing off of this central hub.

"Why?" Naomi can guess, but her head's still buzzing with the events of the day. She rubs her forehead, careful not to reach back and grip her neck. "Please use small words in your explanation."

Alycia smiles, clearly amused.

"We're in a hospital, and you couldn't find one person to give you an Advil?"

"I didn't ask anyone. They—"

"Yeah. Yeah. They have better things to do," Alycia finishes, rolling her eyes. Leaning over the front desk, she addresses the nurse. "Excuse me. Do you happen to have any Advil? My friend has had a rough day."

"She just signed the release papers, right?" inquires the nurse.

Naomi starts to nod then thinks better of it and lets Alycia do the talking.

"Yes. Why does that matter?" Alycia asks.

The nurse smiles cheerfully.

"Because it means she's no longer a patient, and I can give her something from my personal stash." She ducks low under the desk and emerges with two red and white pills in her hand. "Sorry, I only have Tylenol."

"I'm not picky," says Naomi. After accepting the pills, she thanks the nurse.

"My pleasure," says the nurse. "You can grab some water from the cooler over there. You want the right knob for cold water. You'd be surprised how many people mess that up."

"I'll get it," Alycia offers.

Naomi considers protesting but stops to take in the busy waiting room. Even though it's spacious, people line every wall and most of the floor space near walls. Doctors, nurses, and a whole host of others dart back and forth across the center space like crazy drivers trying to beat red lights. Crossing to the water cooler becomes a rousing game of live Frogger. Half the cup of water gets spilled when Alycia's arm gets knocked from behind by a small child.

"Welcome back," Naomi greets, reaching to steady her friend.

"Hope you can swallow pills with next to nothing," Alycia says, "because that was madness, and I ain't doing it again. You want more water, we're fighting our way over to that cooler."

"This will do just fine. Thanks," Naomi assures her. Taking a sip of water, Naomi inserts one pill lengthwise and swallows it. She does the same for the second before using the rest of the water to finish washing them down. A thought pops into her head. "How are we getting home? Our cars are at the school."

"Not sure," Alycia says with a shrug. "Let's go make some rounds."

Naomi starts to follow her but stops suddenly.

"How's your husband?"

"He's fine, but I think he's at a hospital on the other side of the county," Alycia answers. "Mercy something or other. He says it's ugly and he can't wait to get food that's not been covered in shrink wrap for a questionable amount of time."

They continue catching up as they pick their way down the hallway Alycia had indicated before. Most rooms overflow with people. They move by these and linger in the ones with just a few people. It's interesting checking in with various students and their families, sometimes meeting them for the first time. They don't even have to ask many questions. Most kids are bursting to tell their stories.

At the end of the long hallway a pair of double doors lead to a section restricted to hospital employees. Another sign next to the restricted one says Intensive Care Unit.

"I wonder who they're working on," says Naomi.

Before Alycia can answer, the doors swing open and both teachers backpedal two steps to stay out of the way. Two nurses wheel a gurney out and turn left. The small figure looks familiar, but the name remains just on the tip of Naomi's tongue.

"It's Sheridan Colt," says Alycia. "She's in Mark's physics class. Don't you remember? He showed us pictures of his students during that bubble lab."

Sadness ambushes Naomi.

"Poor kid. She probably doesn't even know … about Ian."

"What about him?" Alycia asks. "You never did tell me why you ran off during the evacuation."

"I don't know why," Naomi answers honestly. She leans back against the wall and lowers her voice, not wanting to set off a rumor wildfire. "But he's dead."

Alycia's quiet after the announcement.

"How?" she asks eventually.

"He shot himself," Naomi says, still unable to fully believe the truth. "The police shot him too, but I'm pretty sure the head wound killed him."

"Has anybody gotten in touch with their parents?" asks Alycia.

Naomi shrugs.

"I'm sure the police will handle that. There's only Mom to notify. Dad overdosed a year or so ago. We should stay with Sheridan until her mother arrives."

"That's not going to happen," says a weary female voice.

Naomi looks up to see Officer Bonnie Kiernan approaching, hat tucked under her left arm. After appropriate introductions, she presses the police officer for a more thorough explanation to her last statement. The officer gives them both long, measuring looks.

"Everything I say is completely off the record," says Officer Kiernan.

"Everything you say stays with us," Naomi promises.

"We're not reporters, but we get the idea," Alycia says.

"Mrs. Colt is dead." The officer stops speaking for several beats to give them time to process the statement. "The cause of death hasn't been determined yet …."

"But," Naomi prompts.

"I can't say more than that right now," says the officer. "I'm only telling you this much because I've been asked to sit with Sheridan until she wakes up and can answer some questions. I'd like you two to stay as well. A familiar face will do her good when I break the news to her."

"We'll be happy to stay," Naomi answers quickly. Even though neither of them has had Sheridan as a student, they should still be able to fulfill the familiar face role. "See if Mark can join us," Naomi whispers to Alycia.

"Good idea," says Alycia. "I'll make some calls. I think this is way beyond a text message."

A concerned expression crosses Officer Kiernan's features.

"Mark Quint is a physics teacher at the school," Naomi explains. "He has Sherri this year." For some reason, the girl's nickname comes to Naomi once she mentally links the girl to Mark and his photo obsession.

The officer concedes the point with a brief nod and strolls into the private room where the nurses disappeared with Sherri.

"How is she?" Officer Kiernan asks an unseen person.

Naomi and Alycia follow the officer inside.

"I can't discuss a patient's condition with non-family members." The man's answer comes automatically. The shadows under his eyes tell Naomi it's been a long day. His white jacket bears his name.

"I'm not asking for past medical records, Dr. Hollon," says the police officer. "Nothing official. Not yet. The court order for current records and beyond will be in soon enough. What I want to know now is if this kid has a fighting chance of living."

"It's hard to say." Dr. Hollon returns his attention to his laptop. The stylus in his hand scribbles notes furiously. Sliding the stylus into its holder, he looks up and takes in the small audience, attempting a smile. "She's been through a lot, but the surgeries to remove each bullet went well. She needs to rest. The next twenty-four hours will be crucial. Now, if you'll excuse me, I have a lot of other patients to see."

After thanking the doctor for his time, the three settle in to wait beside Sherri. They do an admirable job of sharing the two chairs until a nurse takes pity on them and squeezes in a metal folding chair.

About one hour into their vigil, they take turns calling their family members. They could conceivably each make their calls together, but the turns guarantee that somebody will always be watching over Sherri. Naomi's conversations with her father and brother bear striking resemblances to each other. Both Dad and Kevin start by expressing how glad they are to hear from her before moving into the scolding stage for not returning their calls earlier. Then, predictably, the scolding morphs into veiled orders that she should stay with one of them while Jack is away. Naomi politely declines both offers, but doesn't get released from the conversations without solemn promises to visit each of them soon.

Over the next hour after the phone calls, many people file in and out. Mark drops by and they duck out to have a brief meal with him in one of the hospital's cafeterias. They bring a sandwich and a water bottle back for Officer Kiernan. The conversation progresses well enough to move them to first-name basis.

At eight o'clock, Alycia and Naomi receive official word that the school will be closed for the rest of the week.

A quarter to nine, Naomi's husband calls, and they have a lovely but brief conversation, most of which Naomi spends reassuring him.

Around ten thirty Alycia's husband picks her up from the hospital.

"When does your shift end?" Naomi asks the police officer once they're alone. She rises from her seat for a change of pace.

"Eight," answers Bonnie. She sighs. "I keep hoping that the next minute will be enough rest and she'll wake up. What's your excuse?"

"Much the same," Naomi replies. "My husband is in England. I'm usually okay with my own company, but tonight, this just seemed more ... fitting. I thought somebody would come relieve you by now."

"He tried," says Bonnie. "I have off tomorrow, so I might as well stick it out."

"How long will it take them to investigate?" Naomi wonders.

"Not sure," Bonnie replies. "It honestly depends on how much red tape gets wrapped around the situation. The physical structure can probably be repaired in a few days."

"The emotional structure's going to take a lot longer," Naomi says, finishing the thought.

The machines monitoring Sherri change pitch before Bonnie can add anything else. Several nurses rush in and make a few adjustments. Things eventually settle down much like they did the last three times this happened.

Naomi wills her heart to slow down again.

The false alarm kills the desire for conversation for a time. Eventually, they both fall asleep in the two higher class hospital chairs. It's not a restful sleep though because nurses and doctors keep checking up on the slumbering patient throughout the night.

Upon awakening in the wee hours of the morning, Naomi blinks and stares dully at the still form before her. She's so steeped in the routine that she fails to register the pair of eyes staring back until a small voice breaks the silence.

"What happened?"

Chapter 41:
I Want Answers

Tuesday, 4:22 a.m.
Englewood Hospital and Medical Center
Englewood, New Jersey

"Where's Val? I don't feel good." Sherri Colt has so many questions to ask, but her brain feels like partially mashed potatoes. The room lights have been dimmed in deference to the hour. A clock in front of Sherri declares the time but she's not sure if it's morning or evening. "Where am I?"

She doesn't expect an answer from the woman staring at her since she's too busy wiping at tears to do much besides flick the arm of the woman next to her. This other woman, who's dressed like a cop, springs out of the chair and steps up beside Sherri's bed.

"Sheridan Colt?" asks the policewoman.

"Yes."

Before she can say much else, a nurse strides into the room and fusses over her. Before she leaves, the nurse warns the two women not to tax Sherri with too many questions.

"But I want answers too," Sherri protests to the air. The nurse is long gone by the time she gets the words formed.

"I think we all want answers," says the cop. She's not wearing her hat and some of her blond hair has escaped the bun at the back of her head. "But we'll take it slowly if we need to. I'm Officer Bonnie Kiernan with the Brantford Township Police Department. This is

168

Naomi Harrison-Kensley; she's a teacher at your school. What do you remember about yesterday?" Her gentle tone puts Sherri on edge.

"I don't know," Sherri admits. Everything's a jumbled mess in her head. After taking some time to order her thoughts, she attempts a summary. "I started walking to school but got picked up by Val's mom. We got breakfast at Dunkin Donuts. I went to some classes … and I woke up here." Panic seizes her. She tries to sit up until pain rips through her stomach. It feels like somebody buried a blazing ax in her gut. Collapsing back against the pillow, Sherri clenches her eyes shut until the pain slowly retreats to something tolerable.

"It's fine if you don't remember everything right away," says the teacher. "You might not know me very well because you haven't had chemistry yet. Call me HK. Maybe you'll have me someday. I know of you through your brother."

An image of her brother fills Sherri's mind. He's standing in the front of a classroom—her classroom—pointing a gun at her. The gun doesn't scare her as much as the hatred she sees in his eyes.

"Ian," Sherri murmurs, shivering at the thought of him.

It's just a bad dream.

If she can just talk to him, he can explain everything.

"Where's my brother? Why isn't my mother here?"

The cop and the teacher exchange looks and close ranks on her. The teacher moves to the other side of the bed and picks up one of Sherri's clammy hands.

The cop clears her throat.

"It's best we halt the discussion for the moment," says the policewoman.

Nameless fears grip Sherri hard, making her heart flutter within her chest. The blood pressure readout spikes, bringing Dr. Hollon and a nurse into the room in a hurry.

"I. Need. To. Know," Sherri says between gasps.

"You need to rest," counters Dr. Hollon. He checks her chart and makes a slight adjustment to the IV drip next to her bed.

A warm, drowsy feeling sweeps over her, but Sherri fights it long enough to grip the doctor's arm.

"Please. Somebody talk to me. What happened yesterday?"

"Is she … okay to hear this now, doctor?" asks the cop.

"Only one way to find out," he replies, checking the clock on the wall. "Captain Rischer dropped by earlier with some paperwork and explained the situation. He said he sent you an updated list of facts and things to ask. I need to finish my rounds soon, but I'll stay and monitor her if you wish to proceed now."

The cop nods thanks and retreats a step to catch up on her messages.

Meanwhile, a nurse brings a cup of water and helps Sherri drink half before handing her a wad of tissues. Finally, everything's ready for "the talk." Sherri's eyes start to well up. Her emotions crumble beneath the sea of sympathetic faces surrounding her.

"It's bad," she says, trying to keep her jaw from trembling.

"There's no easy way to tell you this, so I'll just do it, but first, I want you to know that every person in this room wants to help you in every way we can." The cop pauses her speech long enough to draw a deep breath and compose herself. "Yesterday, around two o'clock, your brother went on a shooting spree inside your high school. We don't have the full details yet, but he died sometime later that afternoon. Your mother was informed of these events sometime in the late afternoon and told which hospital you would be taken to. She never made it."

"She's dead," Sherri finishes. Oddly, this part just makes logical sense. Truth be told, her mother had withdrawn from Sherri and Ian sometime soon after the divorce. Hearing of her death causes an ache, but not as much as it should and *that* cuts Sherri deeply. She pulls apart a few of the tissues in her hands. "How did my brother die?"

"That doesn't matter right now," says HK. "I'm sure the police will know more later."

"He killed himself, didn't he?" asks Sherri.

"Why do you say that?" inquires HK.

Sherri tries to smile but doesn't manage it.

"Runs in the family," she says hoarsely. She coughs then winces and dabs at some tears. It only opens the way for a steady stream, but she feels compelled to explain. "Mom and Ian think I'm stupid. I know Dad committed suicide with pills." As the grief builds inside her, a new thought bursts through with a warm beam of hope. "Where's Val? Can I see her?"

Val would know exactly how to comfort Sherri.

"I'll go see if I can find her," offers HK.

The cop holds out a hand to stop HK from leaving.

Sherri sees the answer in every expression and the rest of her world collapses into darkness.

When she returns to consciousness, only HK remains, dozing in a hospital armchair.

The clock reads 8:02, but time doesn't matter. Nothing really matters now.

Val's gone.

The words seem foreign to Sherri, like they were never meant to be part of the English language.

She can't be gone! I won't let her!

Those words don't seem right either. Sherri wants to cling to them, but they slip away.

When she closes her eyes, she sees Val crawling under a desk. Her once white shirt is bright red. Their gazes connect. Bits of paper flutter down between them. All around them people scream and thrash and fall. The chatter of gunfire reminds her of rain. Val comes closer still.

The memory fades completely.

It's not fair! It should be me. He was my brother. He wanted me dead.

"Hey, those thoughts look painful," says HK. "Feel like sharing? Nurse Nina says sharing might help, but otherwise, you should try not to think about anything but recovering."

"Can you stop thinking about it?" Sherri wonders.

"Not for long. I think two minutes is my record so far."

Sherri appreciates HK's admission.

"Penny for those thoughts?" asks HK. She leans forward. "I bet 99% of them are questions. Can't guarantee any answers, but I can make a list and bother people until you get some answers."

"What will happen to me?" Sherri whispers.

My brother's dead. My mother's dead.

These words feel a tad more fitting.

"Your grandmother will be by in a few hours to visit," says HK. "I had a nice conversation with Mrs. Easterwood this morning. She said she would have been by last night, but her normal nurse had a family emergency and couldn't bring her."

"But what happens after that?" Sherri wonders. "Grandma Shauna lives in a retirement village with single room apartments. I … can't go home, can I? There won't be any adults around." Her throat closes painfully and more tears form.

HK comes over and kneels beside the bed so Sherri doesn't have to look up.

"Concentrate on healing. Why don't you take a nap? I'll ask around to get you some answers." Leaning forward, she places a kiss on top of Sherri's head. "Every other worry can wait for another day."

Epilogue:
The Interview

The Fight for Normal

By Rebecca Treddle (RT)

Two weeks ago, a familiar story scrolled across the newsfeeds. Yet another American high school spiraled into a scene of chaos and pain when a student opened fire on several classrooms. The motives may never be fully known, but interviews with acquaintances suggest the young man simply wanted to be remembered for doing something unforgettable. Due to the violent nature of his actions I have chosen to omit his name from this article. Troubled or not, he does not deserve to be rewarded with any sort of fame or infamy.

I'm joined today by two people who were there that day, two people who had their lives changed forever. Naomi Harrison-Kensley (NHK) teaches chemistry at Brantford Regional High School, and Bonnie Kiernan

(BK) is an officer with the Brantford Township Police Department.

RT: Ladies, thank you for taking the time to speak with me today. I know you'd rather we didn't ever meet under such circumstances, but I appreciate your willingness to share your thoughts and experiences with our audience. I'll ask a few general questions meant for you both before moving into individual ones. Let's start with each of you telling a bit about yourselves.

NHK: There's not that much to know. I've taught chemistry classes at the high school for the past five years. For much of the incident, I was locked in a prep room with one of my colleague's classes.

BK: I'm a cop. Have been for a few years. That's all you need to know.

RT: For those of you who don't know, Bonnie and I grew up together. I might have sort of blackmailed her into this little chat. She'll get over it after a few coffee runs with me. She's a stellar cop and a kind soul. The prickly persona she occasionally dons hides a heart of gold.

RT: When did you realize the incident was real, not some sort of drill?

NHK: I didn't know until after the lockdown was called and we heard more gunfire. I think everybody dismissed the first few shots as random noises.

BK: The dispatcher made it abundantly clear the situation was real.

RT: Every tragedy like this throws fuel on the gun control debate. Do either of you have anything to add to that debate.

BK: I carry a gun every day as part of my job. I see nothing wrong with owning guns, but I'm willing to concede that perhaps society should take some stronger steps to keep these tools out of the hands of nutjobs and suicidal, broken kids.

NHK: I have nothing to add to that.

RT: That's surprising, but I can respect that. If you had to pick only three words to describe your emotions about that day, what would you say?

NHK: Terror. Sadness. Regret.

BK: Terror. Disbelief. Determination.

RT: Sorry to break from my established pattern, but I must know: why regret? You didn't cause any of this.

NHK: Maybe helplessness or heartbreak would be better terms. I regret that our society has not only come to this but continues to come to this time and again. Hardly a week passes without news of a shooting death. Ours might have resulted in 17 deaths and 30+ wounded but even an event with one death or one wound is too many.

RT: Naomi, another few questions for you. The room you were in had no deaths, a few wounds certainly, but no deaths. How are you doing? And how did you pull that off.

NHK: I'm recovering well. Thank you. We blocked the doors with textbooks and had the students hunkered down behind more stacks of textbooks.

RT: That's fascinating. What gave you that idea?

NHK: We had to move the textbooks somewhere to even fit the students in the room. I like to think God prompted my procrastination in doing the book inventory.

RT: Well, whatever the cause, we're grateful for it and the miracle that resulted. Speaking of miracles, I heard some people say the death toll was surprisingly low for an incident like this where so many shots were fired. Do either of you have a comment about that?

NHK: Even one life lost is too many.

BK: I can confirm the speculation that one whole classroom of casualties consists of the CPR training dummies.

RT: I'd been wondering about that rumor. Thank you for confirming. Now, if either of you could say one thing to the perpetrator of the incident, what would it be?

NHK: This isn't the answer. No amount of pain inflicted upon others can fix what's wrong in your life. Part of growing up is dealing with these things. That doesn't necessarily mean alone. Everybody needs people to lean on for support.

BK: This isn't going to end well, for anybody.

RT: Bonnie, a little bird told me you negotiated with the perpetrator for a while. Can you describe that for us?

BK: No. I can't really discuss anything related to that. It's an ongoing investigation. Sorry.

RT: No problem. I figured as much, but you can't fault a girl for trying. Naomi, you're not bound by official capacities and investigations and whatnot. You've also had the perpetrator as a student. Can you tell us a little about him? Did you ever suspect he might be capable of such madness?

NHK: Everybody has the capacity for madness, most just have more self-control. He had his troubled moments, but I could name you half-a-dozen who I would have suspected flipping first. Nothing immediately jumped out as a red flag. He did his work, some days. He tolerated his peers, most days. He even had days when he fully engaged in a lesson. That's the trouble with pain. It often masquerades as something else.

RT: Thanks for that thorough answer. Bonnie, you were the one to break the news of this tragedy and some other, more personal tragedies to one of the wounded young ladies. You went so far as to sit by her bedside most of the night even though your shift had ended. What prompted you to go above and beyond the call of duty?

BK: I wanted to be there for her. It's the worst part of the job, but being the bearer of bad news goes with the territory.

RT: And you, Naomi? You stayed with this same young lady too. She wasn't your student. Why would you choose to spend the night beside her hospital bed?

NHK: Many of the other students had friends and family crowding their rooms. This kid had nobody. Her best friend had just died, though I didn't know that at the time. Her father had passed on previously, and her mother and brother were unavailable as well. She needed somebody, as did I with my husband overseas. She could have died at any moment that night. I didn't want her to be alone, so I stayed and prayed for her.

RT: Do you believe your prayers were answered?

NHK: Yes, but I'm definitely not done praying for her yet.

RT: That's right! I almost forgot. A different little bird told me that you and your husband filed papers to become foster parents to this girl.

NHK: You have very thorough sources, Ms. Treddle. Yes, Jack and I had gone through the steps to become foster parents last year then decided it might not be the right time for us.

RT: What changed your mind?

NHK: She did. I know her full story can't be shared here, not yet anyway, but she's an amazingly resilient kid who deserves to be surrounded by loving, supportive people. If Jack and I can be some of those people, we'll jump at the chance.

RT: The floor is yours. Do either of you have any closing comments?

BK: Be vigilant, but don't waste time worrying. The list of things that *could* go wrong doesn't end. That should never stop you from enjoying peaceful moments. Fight for normal, everyday moments with friends and family.

NHK: Things like this should not happen, but they do. Evil is not a disease we're going to cure any time soon, but love can go a long way in healing what was lost and broken. There is good in the world. Sometimes, you have to look hard to find it. We can never let horrible things permanently steal our peace.

RT: Thanks again. This has been an enlightening experience for me.

Below, you'll find a list of those who perished that day along with several of the wounded. Follow the links to their individual profile pages and to find more information about how you can help their families.

Deceased:

The perpetrator – 18, a disturbed young man

Valerie Amber Marquette – 15, loved theater, dancing, and art, saved her best friend's life that day

Daria Rose Richman – 15, loved music, hanging out at the mall, watching movies, taking videos for YouTube, wanted to be a reporter

Crystal Nicole Merton – 14, loved books and soccer

Rachel Paulette Crest – 17, wanted to attend The College of New Jersey to study special education so she could better understand her brother, Able, who has Down Syndrome

Moira Lacey Stern – 14, played every sport she could from the time she could stand up straight, aspired to join the US Olympic track team

Connor Allen Armstead – 15, loved baseball and video games, wanted to be a professional gamer and app designer

Sebastian Erik Fish – 16, loved learning and building, expected to graduate early, already earned acceptance into Brown University with a concentration in Science, Technology, and Society

Curtis Michael Ryman – 17, loved his girlfriend, Melanie, and planned to propose at graduation, would have become a lawyer and probably taken over his father's law firm

Samuel Avery Alverez – 14, loved football, wanted to join the FBI

Juan Carlos Sanchez – 14, loved drawing, wanted to work for Disney

Timothy Asher Trainor – 14, loved baseball, video games, and the Boy Scouts of America, planned to be an engineer

Keith Kellen – 52, security consultant, loved his family, enjoyed fishing

Thomas Mason Buckle – 61, English teacher, loved his wife, two children, two grandchildren, and three cats

Carlton Ambrose Wright – 45, social studies teacher, loved climbing mountains and traveling around the world learning about new cultures

Kimberly Grace Zeeks – 31, English teacher, loved her family, hailed as a hero for calling the lockdown that may have saved countless lives

Ethan Francis Racer – 38, teacher of environmental sciences and forensic science, loved camping with his wife and three small children

Wounded:

Sheridan Brie Colt – 15, suffered multiple gunshot wounds and is recovering at an outpatient facility

Alissa Olivia Trainor – 15, shot in the arm and left shoulder

Kelly Ann Titus – 29, biology teacher, miraculously survived being shot nine times, the bullets were slowed down and/or deflected by a CPR rescue dummy

Maxwell Donald Kessler – 17, loves his dog Max Jr., wants to join the Navy

Silas Bertrand Cantori – 15, likes acting, survived the assault by playing dead

Officer Sean Burgess – 38, first responder, shot in the left leg

Please visit our main website for a complete list of those affected by this tragedy. I don't want it to seem like only the dead matter because that's certainly not the case. All lives matter, and many more than those listed here or on the longer list have been affected. The wounds don't have to be physical to be devastating. A thing like this has the capacity to change everybody. Let us hope that it's a change for the better.

THE END

Thank You for Reading:

This is one of my darkest tales, but I hope you enjoyed the journey anyway. Even tragic situations can offer us bits of levity and light. I'd love to hear your thoughts.

If you'd like to try something more light-hearted, check out my website (juliecgilbert.com). Many stories can be experienced in ebook, paperback, audiobook, and occasionally, hardcover. The audios are awesome because I've worked really hard to hire highly talented narrators.

Hop on the newsletter (https://www.subscribepage.com/n7e8l8) if you want to keep up with life and new release news. Subscribers also get the first crack at exclusive giveaways.

Please consider leaving a review at your favorite retailer. Your opinion matters, and it will help other readers find this story.

Sincerely,

Julie C. Gilbert

Printed in Great Britain
by Amazon

38016493R00106